TAX ME
IF YOU CAN

by

M.H. VESSEUR

TAX ME
IF YOU CAN

A RADIO DETECTIVE

A novel by

M.H. VESSEUR

Vibes Publishing

Published by Vibes

www.mhvesseur.com

www.facebook.com/MHVesseur

Second edition

ISBN 978-94-91908-30-9 (paperback, 2nd edition)

ISBN 978-90-806920-8-4 (Kindle epub with DRM)

ISBN 978-94-91908-31-6 (epub with DRM for Apple iBooks
and Kobo)

Tax Me If You Can

One

Good jokes are hard to find. The harder you try, the harder they seem to resist. This is of no concern to ordinary people, but it's a hard fact of life if you have a professional need for truckloads of wisecracks. Like Carl Pappas, the world's number one bizz jockey: he needed funny lines five days a week when his radio show The Boardroom was broadcast. Just a couple of quality soundbites were enough to spice up the program. For him, the best way to go about it was to relax and think of something completely different, and just wait till a joke popped up. This always happened, sooner or later, and he had learned to leave the first contours of a joke simmering in the back of his head and not to try it out immediately. When spoken, an immature joke could misfire and ruin a perfect day.

Sometimes a joke that comes up in a man's head is downright sexist or filthy, and then it needs to be moderated to meet the demands of one's audience. Carl could be dining with his girlfriend, and suddenly think of a hilarious one-liner, and then, right before telling her, realize that the joke might offend her. She was not the kind of woman who was easily offended, but Carl wanted to treat her with grace. Another way to make a fool of himself was to try out a premature wisecrack on his producer, Hitomi Sakamoto, and get scolded.

So through the years Carl had learned to swallow these sudden outbursts and work on them a little longer, like a composer working on a song. It seemed perfectly plausible to him that someone like Ludwig van Beethoven would come up with a rough idea for a symphony that opened with da-da-da-da-daaaaah, and then later on change that to da-da-da-daaaaah, and call it the Fifth Symphony. Perfectly normal.

So he worked on stuff a lot of the time. Here was a man who had missed planes and weddings simply by standing still because he refused to abandon his train of thought. Of course his train usually brought him to Laughter Station sooner or later. He had conceived ideas in showers and dentist's chairs, during funerals and lovemaking, during dessert and in the middle of dreams.

But in all his years as a professional bizz jockey and conscience of the worldwide business community, Pappas had never before come up with an idea for a wisecrack while standing on water skis, going fifteen kilometers an hour across a bay. This was an all time first. The line welled up as the morning sun was beating down on him. It shone mercilessly, in spite of the early hour, and if it hadn't been for the water splattering up he would have gone back to the yacht and sat in the shade. Pappas was not a very experienced water skier but he was doing just fine. The speedboat towed him along in a nice, slow pace, leaving him with little else to do but hold on. That left the bizz jockey ample time to think about the task ahead: his preparations for another edition of The Boardroom, just two days away. Of course he was supposed to relax on Saturday morning, but once again he couldn't help himself.

"Taxes are like having an affair with a beautiful woman," he said aloud, in the roar of the speedboat engine and the rushing of the water. "First you put in a lot of effort. Then you get rewarded. But finally, you always pay."

He laughed out loud. Not necessarily because the wisecrack was incredibly funny but because no one could hear him. All around him the water in the bay was clear, with its shades of blue and green. He was away from his own city for a couple of days, and even if this was just a business visit, it upped Carl's spirits. Perhaps he should get away from it all more often to allow the ideas to come to him more easily.

Nevertheless, it was the beginning of a statement that could have the right amount of grandeur to kick off next Monday's program. After all, Monday's broadcast of The Boardroom was going to be all about how certain people and businesses succeeded in dodging taxes, and how money was diverted to tax-free paradises like Corazón.

The city of Caribal lay inside an oversized lagoon that protected it from the ocean and gave it a natural harbor. It was a very convenient setting for this capital of the Republic of Corazón, a small nation close to the equator that kept a low profile in the capable hands of a government of generals, middle-aged men who knew best. Most of the people had forgotten the word "junta", as they had once called their revolutionary government. The generals had taken off their uniforms and dressed in friendly white suits, had done away with the Wayfarer sunglasses and had actually done their utmost to raise the standard of living to comfortable levels. There had even been elections at irregular intervals. The Republic of Corazón had come a long way, even pleasing the United Nations to some extent. If there were any unpleasantries, they had to do with drug trafficking in the tropical rainforest that surrounded Caribal and which covered almost the entire country stretching way beyond its borders into the rest of the continent.

In front of Carl Pappas the speedboat was making a wide turn through the passage that connected the bay to the ocean, past the cliffs rising from the water a hundred meters high. The cliffs were mainly topped with a rich foliage of rhododendrons and palm trees, only occasionally interrupted by a large villa. It was the neighborhood of Corazón's privileged and they were living too high above the water to probably even hear Carl Pappas' shout as he sped over something big floating on the waves.

He lost his balance and fell, headfirst into the ocean. He came back to the surface, gasping for air. The speedboat was moving away from him, the towrope jumping in the water behind it. They didn't look back.

They'll start missing me in a minute, Carl thought.

Then he remembered the collision. He unbuckled his skis and pushed them in the water in front of him as he swam back a little, following the trail he had made before it dissolved. It was only a few meters.

Right before him a dead man floated on his back, eyes wide

open, staring at the tropical dome above him.

Two

Sometimes you can't keep your mouth shut and there you go. You don't have to be a bizz jockey, but it helps. Live radio always does something to the adrenalin stream in any man's body, and certainly Carl Pappas' — though he had learned to restrain himself a little bit over the years. But every once in a while "it" happened and most of the time it was primarily embarrassing. This time, however, it turned out to be quite an enterprise. In the end Hitomi Sakamoto had the last say in the matter. And it was because she agreed that they all ended up in Corazón, but that's no reason to blame her. It was Carl who had started it all.

The live broadcast of The Boardroom was in full swing. The president of a large government fiscal institution was the special guest star and the bizz jockey had been pushing him to say something about the latest statistics, which showed how the wealthiest citizens paid the least amount of taxes. Of course this had not really been news, but finally there were some new figures and they were staggering.

"Staggering is not the right word," said Carl. "It's more like taking the elevator four kilometers down the mineshaft. It is physiologically impossible to pay less taxes than these people. Surely the government is planning to take a position on this?"

"You are pushing something towards the government that is really the responsibility of our society's elite, Carl," said Hector Kopenhagen, officially introduced as the Secretary of the Treasury, a man with a voice deep and snarling enough to make a lasting impression on even the crankiest transistor radio. He would have made an even more lasting impression had The Boardroom been a TV show, with his pale smoker's complexion, his thick-rimmed glasses and his eyebrows that rose from his forehead like the wings of a blackbird.

"Ow come on!"

"No really. We are talking about the upper layer. It is not the government's duty to highlight their behavior when it comes to paying taxes. They are the government. They vote. They have a powerful representation in the capital, they lobby every part of the government. No, it is you who should act."

Behind the glass of the control room, sound engineer Don Wozniak smiled. As usual he was surrounded by the remains of coffee-dipped doughnuts and paper cups with cold coffee, which stood dangerously close to WCBN Radio's expensive studio equipment. His thick lips were shining from something fat he had recently been eating, and sugar stained his T-shirt. His humongous glasses gave him a puppet like quality, as if he stepped right out of the Thunderbirds and someone was pulling his strings. If any pulling of strings was going on, it would have to be done by the radio show's producer Hitomi Sakamoto, who was standing next to the sound engineer. Don pushed his elbow towards Hitomi's thighs, but she quickly moved her hip to avoid the intentional collision. Her face radiated disgust at the idea alone. Fortunately she had the reactions of a cat, so moving around the hulk of the sound engineer was never a problem for her. Most of Hitomi's few hours away from working on The Boardroom she spend either in the open air jogging along the city river or in a park, or in the gym working on maintaining the tightness of her slim Japanese body. Though in her forties now, she remained much younger than other women her age, and because of the shape she was in she was immune to jokes about her advancing years. Don Wozniak was much younger, but that was a useless advantage in the presence of Hitomi's natural force. "I can hear her six pack," he used to say to Carl Pappas when they were alone and she couldn't hear them. But for Don, that was not jealousy. It was merely a sign of respect.

"That's gonna shut him up for the first time since you slipped him that note saying that Neil Armstrong had died," Don chuckled.

And it did. Carl sat for a moment, long enough for everybody in the studio — and a large chunk of the audience of The Boardroom — to notice he was momentarily at a loss of words.

"Got you there, eh, Carl?" said Hector Kopenhagen.

The bizz jockey took the deepest breath, close to the microphone, to make sure everybody heard it, and exhaled even louder. "Of course you got me there, Mr. Secretary. I'm speechless. Last time I checked, you were responsible for the tax agency. You are the boss here. And suddenly it's my problem?"

"It's a question of ethics, Carl. The people's representatives do not want the rich to pay more taxes. The representatives themselves are mostly members of the upper class."

"Are you?"

"Well... Yes. But that's not the point. I pay more tax than I'm supposed to, I'm giving the example. That's the only thing I can do. However, I am not in a position to ask people to change their behavior, to change the focus of their lobby to keep taxes low for wealthy folks, because I'd be kicked out of my job first thing next morning. But you can do it, Mr. Pappas. You can appeal to the people and start a rally. You can start a movement, start a new awareness. Almost all of us were smoking fifty years ago, even on live television. That's gone now. It took a while, but it worked. Perhaps it's time for a new movement."

"I'm speechless again, Mr. Secretary. You're a smooth operator."

"Got you there again, Carl. It's really not such a big deal. A bigger problem is this: there's still too much money leaking away to certain countries, certain tax-free paradises."

"You referring to tropical paradises with bank secrecy? Nameless bank accounts on the beach?"

"Yeah. These people are laughing at you, Mr. Pappas."

Hitomi noticed the sudden shift from Carl to Mr. Pappas.

That's a sign, she thought. For a moment, she was worried that Don Wozniak would try to touch her again with his elbow, but he hadn't noticed the sudden shift in the live mood.

"Laughing?"

"Yeah. They're all laughing, I know, because you talk about this stuff a lot but you never act. So you're becoming a toothless tiger."

"A toothless tiger?"

Behind the glass, Don cursed. "That guy had better watch his tongue."

"It's just getting interesting, Don Lech Wozniak," whispered Hitomi. She could feel something coming.

"I admit to being a toothless tiger myself," said Secretary Kopenhagen. "At least to a certain extent I lack power. But you... People are talking, so I've heard, about your easy life, talking about precarious topics like this, the way the business community behaves, but you never put your money where your mouth is. You would be the last man to go to a tax-free paradise and stand up, now wouldn't you, Mr. Pappas?"

How very, very clever, thought Hitomi. This man is actually challenging Carl Pappas and it looks like the bizz jockey is going to fall for it. She couldn't suppress a smile, and at the same time she felt for Carl and his upcoming, uncontrollable anger.

And she had a point on both accounts.

"It's a good thing this ain't a music show, Mr. Secretary, because then I'd have put on a couple of Frank Zappa records that would make your hair stand on end because of their explicit lyrics. You want to take me to a fight? Is that it? Are you going to sit here and call me a wussy? Is that it? You think I'm afraid to go where the money is and kick them all in the butt because you are unable to do that? Well let me tell you something before my sound engineer unplugs both of us because no cursing's allowed on The Boardroom. Man you're boiling my blood here. No one gets away with calling me a coward. Do you want to take back what you just said, Mr.

Secretary, or do you stand by your opinion?"

"You can't frighten me, Mr. Pappas. I stand."

"Good. We're getting out now for some messages from our sponsors. I need to get some fresh air, and when we get back we'll just change the subject. But this I promise you: you will come back to swallow your words."

"Very good. We need people like you."

Then they were off the air. The voice of Don Wozniak announced there was a five-minute recess for commercials. Carl jerked off his headphones and walked out of his radio temple.

Secretary Kopenhagen just sat and smiled.

And Hitomi, she smiled too.

Three

Carl Pappas had arrived on the *Rising Sun*, the yacht of Moon Afficionades, a billionaire's son and a friend of Hitomi Sakamoto. Carl's radio producer Hitomi had been waiting for him. Soon after, while Carl was preparing for his water ski trip, one of the government officials arrived to pay him a visit. A small vessel moored alongside the large, white pearl of the seas. A man in a business suit energetically climbed the rope ladder that hung from the stern. He was obviously a man in good health, a man who exercised.

"Mr. Carl Pappas, welcome to Corazón!" said the man. "I am Colonel Rhodes, Minister of the Economy of the Republic. I have convinced my fellow cabinet ministers that you are an *amigo* of the Republic and of the revolution."

"Thank you Colonel," said Carl. "Are you by any chance related to the late Cecil Rhodes of Rhodesia?"

There was an awkward silence. Hitomi Sakamoto, in one of her fine performances as guardian of the great bizz jockey, broke the spell by laughing out loud. Moon Afficionades joined, and then Colonel Rhodes, and finally Carl himself.

"Of course I am an *amigo* of your wonderful country," said

Carl. "How could I not be? In a moment I'll be skiing this incredible bay, before getting to work. I take it you didn't have a hard time convincing them?"

"There were some people with second thoughts," said Colonel Rhodes and he smiled a many-faceted smile: it could mean virtually anything.

To the bizz jockey however, it meant very little. He was used to smiles like this.

"There are people," said the Minister of Economy, Colonel Rhodes, "who are worried about your presence here, and especially the presence of members of your radio crew. Rumor has it that you are doing a live broadcast from the city of Caribal."

"That's not a rumor," Carl said. "We have a stack of permits from your authorities. One for almost everything we do here, including sleeping and waterskiing, which I am about to undertake."

"Permits are a private matter between you and the government, Mr. Pappas. Well, at least in our country. But I am delighted to hear you are going to enjoy your stay in our wonderful bay to the fullest. And I will surely not keep you from it. It's just that I am curious about the topic of your radio show. Will it be the booming business of Corazón perhaps? Or are you going to take on the contrabandistas operating in our jungles on the Plato Grosso?"

"We mean to keep that a surprise. It's hard enough to keep our presence here from our audience. Let's not spoil their appetite for Monday night, shall we?"

Colonel Rhodes looked towards the sea. If he was annoyed by Pappas' blatant refusal to open up in this inquiry, he certainly hid it well. He inhaled deeply, exclaiming: "Smell that ocean, *amigo*. Such a young day and already so lovely!"

He was a tall, robust man. Tanned, with long black whiskers and superior eyebrows above piercing dark eyes. He wore a business suit, an almost white, expensive piece of tailoring; all of it gave him the looks of a movie star. A man with an oversized tan and teeth a bit too white for his age. But like all members of the local junta he no longer wore sunglasses, and that gave him a certain amount of vulnerability and accessibility, although that was probably a complete mirage.

"Are you a beach man, Mr. Pappas?" said Rhodes, as he pointed towards a long stretch of white sands on the left side of the city of Caribal.

The city and this beach were the only places where one could go ashore. Beyond that, the coast was all high cliffs, shooting up a hundred meters high or more. Behind the white beach, the dark green forest stood like a wall, its canopy stretching inland for a couple of hundred meters. Beyond, the trees shot upwards on the cliffs, towards the Plato Grosso, the high plateau that dominated this part of the world for thousands of kilometers.

Colonel Rhodes took a pair of binoculars that stood on a table and peeked towards the sand. "Are you a ladies' man? Lots of beautiful ladies here in Caribal. Beach is full of them, even at this early hour. Why not cancel your show and have the time of your life? I'm sure if you say you're the Bizz Jockey, women will fall for you immediately."

"I very much doubt that, Colonel. Besides, at my age I'd look silly on a beach in swimming pants, surrounded by twenty-somethings."

The Colonel laughed and put the binoculars in Carl's hands. "Nonsense. Here. Take a look. Look at the coast and take it in for a moment."

Shrugging, Carl obliged. He took a quick look and then put the binoculars away. "You've convinced me, Colonel."

The tall man, who succeeded at not sweating at all, in spite of the closeness of the sun, bent over to the bizz jockey. "Always keep a sharp eye on the coast, *amigo*." Again he shot Carl that probing look.

"A word of advice then, Mr. Pappas," said Rhodes. "If I were you..."

"Which you're not," said Carl with a big smile.

"If I were you I'd take on any topic, and that's *any* topic you like, except the drug trafficking. These people, well, they're beyond our control and they're very violent. One of the reasons the people of Corazón are comfortable with our military government is that everybody leaves everybody pretty much alone. We do not bend to foreign pressure to wage an everlasting war on drugs, and that saves us. There are no killings and there is hardly any corruption. Yes, maybe our leader is a dictator, but in many countries you can see what comes after the removal of the dictator: total ruination. Kick out the top brass and you end up in the hands of a population that cannot agree on anything. Just take a look at Baghdad, at Cairo. Need I say more? People can see we are doing well. It would be a regrettable mistake to focus the world's attention on a few leaf-smuggling farmers and stir things up, wouldn't you say?"

The Colonel took Pappas' hand and shook it.

"Aren't you basically saying that you wish to censor my show, Colonel?" said Carl.

They looked into each other's eye for a moment. Carl saw the head of Hitomi peek around a mast, but she was too far away on the yacht to have heard any of the conversation. Moon Afficionades' family yacht *Rising Sun* was large enough to take twenty people on board for long voyages, and that excluded the crew. It was a fast ship, designed for sailing but also for stealing the show in any high society harbor anywhere, with its astonishing good looks. Hitomi and Moon were standing somewhere near the front bow, Carl and the Colonel were on the afterdeck.

"No. I understand your paranoia, Mr. Pappas. Many foreigners are still skeptical about the way we run this country. Be that as it may, things function quite properly here. We have less violence than many large, modern Western countries. I have learned that censorship only creates a feeling of uncertainty, of danger even."

The Colonel waved to the helmsman of the small boat that had brought him aboard earlier. "So you are a free man, Mr. Bizz Jockey. I wish you a good time here in our beautiful country and I hope you consider yourself my *amigo*."

He gave Carl a business card. "If you run into problems, do call me. I consider it my personal responsibility that you fare well and that whatever business you are doing, you do it successfully. And I must say I admire your stamina. You flew in late last night and you're already up and running and getting ready to water ski. You go ahead and enjoy." Then he started climbing off the ladder, assisted by the helmsman, downwards to the little transport vessel. "And remember," he said, once he got down, "to always keep an eye on the shore. There are nice girls, but there are also lots of nasty rocks!"

"I am confident I can tell one from the other," yelled Carl as the transport vessel started to sail away from the yacht, picking up speed.

"I am sure he means well," said Hitomi, who suddenly turned up next to her boss.

"These junta boys always have strange ways of bringing their message. They say lots of stuff and then leave you to the puzzle," said Pappas. "So now I'll be watching the shore for the rest of the day."

Hitomi looked puzzled for a moment, then she turned to her boss. "Taking on a tax fugitive's paradise like Corazón is already drawing attention. I got the word that even the board at WCBN Radio is getting calls and pressure."

"I'm not taking on Corazón, Hitomi. We're taking on injustice. It's very important that I stress that during the broadcast: it's the problem in general. We're basically here for the weather. And the beaches, of course."

Four

In the midst of the hassle of policemen and soldiers running across the decks of the *Rising Sun*, police barges and a military ship floating all around them and a helicopter hovering in the air, Carl Pappas remembered that one line: *Always keep an eye on the shore.* Such a strange thing to say. And with such emphasis. What had Colonel Rhodes meant?

Carl decided to follow this piece of peculiar advice. There was nothing he could do now anyway. The investigation was in full bloom and they were not allowed to leave before things were wrapped up. The police concluded that the dead man in the water must have drowned by accident, so all they did now was check the identity of everybody involved and make sure they got the details right. In a matter of minutes the whole show would be over. The body of the unknown man had already been brought ashore.

Standing on the starboard side of the *Rising Sun*, Carl raised the binoculars and looked at the coast. He ignored the beach that Colonel Rhodes had been pointing out. Instead he looked at the high coast closest to the place where the dead man had been floating. They were cliffs with a capital C, no doubt about it.

The sun was climbing to its peak fast and poured melted gold over the lagoon and the ocean. But the cliffs seemed untouched by this. They stood cold and solid in the ocean and carried a forest of rhododendrons and villas and swimming pools on their tops, high up there. From where Pappas was standing, however, most of what was up there remained beyond eyesight. All he could see was cliffs and rhododendrons and palm trees, and occasionally some white walls or windows or roof, or the edge of a terrace marked by parasols.

Pappas had heard enough about the Republic of Corazón to know that the country thrived as an international financial hub, a good haven for companies and wealthy individuals who wanted to stay out of the mainstream and avoid attention. There were no paparazzi here; they were simply denied access. That was about the only unusual thing about the country. There was a small group of powerful rich people, mostly living on top of the cliffs overlooking the ocean. Eighty percent of the population was certainly not rich, but they were not living in slums either. There was free schooling for all children and free medical care for all citizens. The wealth of Corazón was as visible as that of a Middle-East oil state.

"You wealthy buggers," murmured the bizz jockey. He meant no offense. To him, the lifestyle of the rich and famous was funny in a way that eluded the rich and famous themselves. In Corazón, people displayed their wealth like in any other place. Not only were their houses the most expensive around, they were also built on the most expensive spots: the hard-to-reach top of the cliffs shielding the Plato Grosso from the ocean. Getting swimming pool tiles up there was an enterprise all on its own. The good side of it was that everybody could clearly see them up there. One could stand in any Caribal city square, stand anywhere on the beach, stand anywhere on any boat in this area, and clearly see the white villas up there, shining in the sun like crowns.

Carl focused on the villa right above the spot were he had skied over the dead man. The rock formations were erratic. First a couple of cliffs rose from the water in the shape of shark teeth: long and thin and bent. They were perhaps thirty to forty meters high and it was possible to sail a small boat between them. Beyond these tooth-shaped rocks, the coast rose like a wall, almost completely vertical, with only a few bushes sprouting from the rock surface, places for seagulls to hide.

More than a hundred meters above sea level the rock wall ended and gave way to the beginning of the forest canopy. Surrounded by the rich greenness of the rhododendrons and palm trees stood a large white villa. Closest to the edge was a white terrace with sunscreens and, probably, a swimming pool. Behind that a glass wall rose, two stories high, and above that was a balcony as wide as the house — dozens of meters wide — and a brown roof.

"You're killing me softly with your house," murmured Carl. He was a successful entrepreneur and he got paid handsomely for his disc jockey talents, and his accountant had assured him that he could retire at will now, but the price of this nice little owl's nest would probably be a little bit too high for him.

He liked the ambiance though. It felt like a James Bond movie set.

Then he spotted a man on the balcony. The man stood there, looking also through binoculars. It was not a coincidence, for the man kept his eye straight on the *Rising Sun*. He was looking back at Carl Pappas.

Five

Moon Afficionades was adamant.

"I am leaving," he said after the police invasion had come to an end and they were alone on the *Rising Sun* again. "All according to plan, I might add."

"Are you chickening out?" yelled Carl.

"It's difficult enough to get permits for this place as it is. I have to be gone today and if I don't, I have to apply for the right papers all over again."

"Can't you just pay someone?" said Hitomi.

"I resent that," said Moon.

"Oh come on, Moon," said Hitomi. "The Republic of Corazón welcomes all foreign wealth at all times. As a member of the Afficionades family and consortium they know exactly who you are and they'll give you your permits before you can even ask."

"All wrong, my dear Sakamoto-san. They want to avoid all suspicion of favoritism. That's why permits are very difficulty to obtain here."

"Permits are hardly ever refused when your family name is Afficionades."

"Yes. Listen guys, it's been my pleasure giving you shelter, but I must leave now. A corpse in a military dictatorship is a tricky thing; I'd rather not stick around. If my family has business interests here, I'd rather not get involved in anything tricky. Just go to the Grand Corazón and you'll be fine. I'll call to make sure you'll be received honorably."

The *Grand Corazón* had been built a long time ago by some foreign colonial power, but it had lost none of its splendor. Since newfound wealth had elevated the small Republic, its new owners had invested heavily and now the hotel was the crown of the city. Once it had even stood in the shadows of the government palace. But that building had been partially damaged during the Revolution a couple of decades ago, and had been turned into a public garden. The remaining walls stood quietly together with the palm trees. Mothers, children and dogs played among the fountains. The generals had retreated to an uninteresting office building that suited the modesty they wished to display.

Of course the *Grand Corazón* was a more suitable place to proceed with the preparations for the next broadcast of The Boardroom, which was to be done live after the weekend. Hitomi Sakamoto had already been here for a couple of days, to take care of the organizational aspects of the operation. She was accompanied by several editorial assistants. Early Monday morning, staff writer and main supplier of texts for the bizz jockey, Job Messner, would arrive just in time to come up with the necessary impromptu lines. There was no need for Job to be here earlier, since he had to wait till all the content for the show was lined up properly. Flying to the Republic of

Corazón with Job would be WCBN Radio managing director Phil Solo, who would from then on be in charge. Which would mean little more than sit in the sun, because with Hitomi around everything was already taken care of.

From his private suite Carl Pappas made a call to a specific number that paged Mach One. Within minutes the hotel phone rang and a receptionist connected him through.

"Good Lord, Pappas, you've barely arrived in that shady country and already somebody's dead," said the low, slow voice of the mysterious middle man.

"Feelin' funny today, Mach? Listen, I know you're busy working for my Monday show, but I got another job for ya." Carl didn't even begin to ask how Mach One could already have known about the corpse in the bay; such things were simply typical for this mysterious man with the hat and the scarred upper lip and the history of unmentionable adventures. From the cold war to modern cybercrime: you name it and Mach One had been there.

But now, the man mainly coughed.

Carl thought he also heard the sound of Mach's rumpled raincoat.

The man's a museum piece, he thought. He hasn't changed his act since Peter Falk first played *Columbo* on TV.

"You need to quit smoking, Mach. Think about me for a minute. If you die, who is going to do all the deep background research for me? Huh?"

"I'll be the last man smoking. What will you be?"

"Listen, I need to know who that dead guy in the bay was and I need to know it real fast."

"It's a military dictatorship, Pappas. People die in places like that for no reason. What significance could it possibly have for you? You'll be there for three days and then you get out. Basta." Another coughing fit.

"I can't say."

"You can't say?"

There was an unwritten agreement that Mach One might keep things secret from Carl Pappas, but that Carl Pappas would never hold anything from the Mach.

"I can't say, because I don't know. I have a bad feeling about this," said Carl, deliberately using one of Mach One's favorite lines from the movies.

"That can't be good," said Mach One, reciprocating with another movie line. "Do elaborate, please."

"I looked up, through binoculars, to the villa right above the place where we found the dead guy. Huge house. I saw a man standing on the balcony looking straight at me, also through binoculars. We looked at each other for a minute and then he went inside the house."

"So?"

"I think he smiled at me."

"You're nuts, Pappas. Has anyone told you, you're nuts?"

"Not yet, but I'm sure it will come to that soon. Just check it out, OK? I've checked the exact location, more or less, on the internet and I'll send you an image, if you give me a number. I need to know who the dead guy was and who lives in that house."

Mach One could clearly be heard sighing on the other end of the line. That could mean shortage of breath as much as irritation at the request.

"I'm already on it."

Carl went down to the pool to relax for a while and get some coffee. As soon as he sat down by the bar, someone patted his shoulder.

"Well of all the people in the world, if that's not Carl Pappas, the Bizz Jockey himself! Look Margareth, it's the man," a loud voice said.

Carl turned and saw two bronzed, middle-aged people, dressed in expensive clothes, manicured and perfumed, with white teeth and jewels, and not a pound overweight.

"Barman, this man's drinks are on me," said the man, his hand still on Carl Pappas' shoulder. "I'm Roland Gabrielos by the way, and this is my wife Margareth."

Carl hesitated, then nodded. "OK, thank you. How are you?"

They shook hands, which meant that Carl's shoulder was finally released.

"Do I know you?"

The man burst into a laugh that sounded like an automatic rifle. "Does he know me! That's a laugh. Well, you may not remember me, but I do remember being on your show."

"I'm really sorry," said Carl.

"Oh that's alright. All these guests you host... why would you remember them all? I was just an incidental guest on the radio, ten years ago, of course you don't remember me." Roland Gabrielos bent over slightly to Carl. "Listen, are you here for your pension too?"

Carl took a more relaxed pose on the barstool and looked across the pool and towards the ocean. "My pension?"

"Sure," Gabrielos said, with a very soft voice now. Even his wife would not be able to hear him, but then again, she was looking around anyway, at the people around and in the pool. "I've moved seventy-five percent of my assets to one of the banks here in Caribal over the years and I'm paying only two percent taxes. My middle man has put a cloak on the transferring of my funds. Made them look like business activities. I'm sittin' pretty from now on. We spend part of the winters here, for the climate of course, but also to check on the funds here."

While he had carefully been listening, Carl felt irritation rise. It resembled nausea. He recognized an upcoming anger that needed to be suppressed at all cost. He had learned long ago that surrendering control to anger was too dangerous. He had damaged reputations and damaged his own position by letting anger flow out without any restraint. It was not good for The Boardroom. Hell, he was here because he had lost his temper to begin with! It was better to let the anger subside, and then fake it.

So he listened a while longer and then interrupted the man. "Don't you feel you are depriving the economy of your homeland by not paying proper taxes?"

The man laughed again.

Cheerful fellow, Carl thought.

"I knew you were going to ask me something like that. But I guess that's just an occupational hazard. It's just a reflex, right? You bark a cynical remark faster than you can think, right? Hey, Margareth, the man's an actor."

"Yeah, right," said Carl, and he smiled.

What the heck, he thought. I'm not getting into a public

debate here. No Don Wozniak around to cut off the microphone of this guest speaker!

"It's easy," said Gabrielos. "Listen. The government's been overspending since 1970 and you're telling me I'm depriving them of my money. Ha! That's a laugh. I'm doing the right thing here. Keeping my hard earned money out of the hands of a spendthrift government."

"Your government is not spendthrift," said Carl, barely able to control his anger. "Who uses that word anymore, *spendthrift*? The only person to go on record as being spendthrift was Liberace! And you're right, there's nothing wrong with bringing your money to safety, but paying only two percent taxes is ridiculous. What about the education of the next generations? What about keeping medical care available for people who are not rich like you? What about the need for the government to invest in future technologies? What about roads? Have you thought about that? Can't you at least double the digits here? Is it so terrible to pay, say, ten percent?"

"Give the man a drink, bartender," brawled Gabrielos.

"Easy, dear," his wife Margareth whispered.

"I'm easy like Sunday morning, darling. I don't have to take this from anyone. I gave five million away to charity for crying out loud. So do a lot of other people."

"That only helps to make you feel good about yourself, but it is entirely besides the point. I'm not saying you should pay taxes as if it were charity. We all have obligations towards society. Some are collective."

"Listen, Mr. Bizz Jockey, you want me to pay taxes? You want me to volunteer and bring my money to the slaughterhouse without a fight? Well, I dare you. Tax me if you can!"

Carl couldn't suppress a big grin. "Well spoken, Roland. I can see why I had you for a guest in my show."

"It doesn't matter what I think, Pappas. I'm an old geezer, I'm a success of the past. Look around you, see all these young people? Go ahead, look."

Gabrielos was right. There were a lot of people here that were much younger than him. Twenty-somethings. Thirty-somethings.

"Now that you mention it."

"They're the new generations of millionaires and billionaires from Silicon Valley and all these high-tech places. Young kids who suddenly got rich after selling another social media platform." As he spoke, Gabrielos waved around him excessively.

"I thought these kids were likely to follow the example of Bill Gates and give away some money," Carl objected.

"They're here, I tell you. Well, what do you want to drink? Want what I'm having?"

He pointed to a glass with an orange substance it in, on the thinnest glass leg imaginable.

"No, I'll just have a strong coffee. I feel I'm going to be needing it."

"Don't tell me you're here to work."

"Right, let's not."

Six

The lobby of the *Grand Corazón* was large enough to receive the entire troupe of the Bolshoi Ballet, including their entourage and secret police, and still leave room for catering personnel. It was divided into many sections by potted plants and palm trees, which created ample space for private meetings and telephone calls. As a producer, Hitomi Sakamoto liked being in large spaces with a lot of people. It spiraled her adrenalin levels and that came in handy when you had to do a lot of stuff in a very short time.

When Carl arrived in the sitting corner behind a bush of plants, Hitomi was just shoving a monologue down her cell phone.

"I know that, Phil, but I am concerned about Carl's safety. No matter what they say here, it's still a military junta. When push comes to shove, they can do anything and then deny it all and there'll be nothing you can do about that."

Hitomi gestured to Carl while she switched the cell phone to its speaker.

"Relax, Sakamoto," shouted Phil Solo from the other end of the line. "Who the f*!# promoted you Chief Security Officer of

WCBN Radio? You take care of The Boardroom and I take care of the rest. Capiche? I've spoken to my old pal in the government of Corazón and there is nothing to worry about."

"Who's your old pal here, Phil?" said Carl, making a face that could have been an imitation of a crying Stan Laurel — or a laughing one, for that matter.

"Ah, Carl, I'm glad you're there. There is no arguing with your producer. I talked to Pedro Rhodes and he assures me we're sittin' pretty. He's in line with the government's top brass, so that includes the police and the army."

"Pedro Rhodes, huh."

"The topics of Monday's broadcast must by now be known to the top brass here," said Hitomi, now fully annoyed. "They're not going to be amused."

"Get off your rock, Sakamoto," said Solo. "It's time for the Republic of Corazón to be taken seriously by the world. Part of their strategy is through scrutiny by the public eye. The tax evasion problem is bothering the government. It makes them rich but it also holds the danger of becoming an international pariah. Everybody needs the involvement of an authority like the Bizz Jockey to deal with that tax thing. Get it? Carl is a neutral party from the outside. They are confident that things will work out, even if the first response is not good. So you guys just stay cool, don't mingle in local affairs unless they're relevant to the program and I'll be seeing you on Monday."

Hitomi Sakamoto picked up the cell phone to talk about some details and then put it away. "No problem there, BJ. If we take Solo's word for it."

"I see no reason not to. We're his chicken with the golden eggs. If we were in danger he'd be here by Concorde before you could repeat the question."

"Concorde has been out of business since 2003, Carl," said Hitomi.

"Yeah, right."

"What's more important: how's the inside information? Will it be here on time? I'm getting a little bit worried here. I had to beat around the bush with Solo, make him believe we're on the right track. Truth of the matter is we have a lousy show so far. You need to come up with some shocking stuff and you've got precious little time to accomplish that."

Carl plunged into one of the leather armchairs. "Haven't you been listening to what the man said? You need to relax. It will be here. And I disagree with you about having a lousy show. We've got plenty of stuff. On Monday, Job will do his thing and it will all sound crisp and new."

"If you say so," said Hitomi, looking emotionless.

"You just don't like me having a source that you don't control," said Carl. "I'm sorry about that. I cannot change it."

"I've learned to live with that," said Hitomi. "It's the bizz jockey's prerogative as far as I'm concerned. Just don't pretend for a minute that I don't know that you've put your personal secret agent on the job again." She opened a small suitcase, took out some papers and gestured to two of her editorial assistants who were sitting in another corner. The mere fact that her boss used an outsider unknown to her, annoyed Hitomi, but she usually ignored it because she felt you can't win every battle in life.

"I'll pretend I didn't hear you say that," said Carl.

The assistants came rushing towards her. Joining them was a hotel receptionist.

"Mr. Carl Pappas of WCBN Radio?"

"Uh... yes?"

The man handed him a cordless hotel phone. "A call for you, Sir. Kindly return the handset to reception when you're through." He walked away.

Carl got up and walked away with the phone, in the general direction of nowhere.

"Carl Pappas."

"Pappas, things are not looking good."

"Mach One. Once again you're fast as lightning. Don't tell me you got answers already," said Carl, suddenly standing still in the middle of the lobby.

Someone bumped into him, so he stepped into another quiet corner and sat down. "OK, let's have it, Mach."

"Turns out the dead guy is the man who was going to deliver you the information, acting on my orders," said Mach One. He talked softly now, in a conspiratory tone.

"Oh dear."

"He was going to bring you a CD-ROM with bank account numbers and names of several key figures from the worldwide business community who have parked large amounts of money there," Mach One continued. "Hardcore tax evasion proof, Pappas. It was supposed to include figures about their tax evading behaviors. Some of it illegal, some of it legal. But all of them get away with paying much less tax than other citizens of many rich countries, exactly the point you wanted to make."

"That's just great, Mach. Not only am I not going to get the data, your man has probably been killed! This can't be an accident."

"Very unlikely, I'd say. Because I've also checked the ownership of the house you were talking about."

At that moment, a shadow fell over Carl. He looked up and saw Colonel Rhodes hovering over him. The man looked far from amused.

The coffee tasted excellent. They were sitting in a VIP room of the *Grand Corazón*, where the chairs were even more luxurious.

"I'm worried about your safety, Mr. Pappas," said Rhodes. "Eh… Is it alright if I call you Carl?"

"Why of course! I hope you don't mind if I continue calling you Colonel. It sounds… appropriate."

"As you wish. I have received word that you discovered a corpse in the bay. How unfortunate. As it turns out, the deceased has a shady record, I'm afraid."

"Shady?"

"An industrial spy of sorts. I'm not sure. Our country is still looked upon with much scrutiny, Carl. Several governments have been trying to infiltrate our businesses and governments and banks. This man… Well, it seems he has been prying around locally for a while. Our secret police chief says he was on to him."

"I don't see why that should concern me or my safety. Remember, my waterskiing trip hadn't been planned. It was an impromptu affair. So I skied over the guy by accident, you see? Could have been anybody."

"But it hasn't been *anybody*, Carl. At least I don't think so. The man has been looking into banking affairs in the capital. We have reason to believe he has gained access in an illegal way. And now... all of this happens precisely in the weeks before you are holding your great live broadcast about the financial matters of the Republic of Corazón. I see a pattern there."

"That's just speculation, General... Pardon me, I mean Colonel. I don't see that pattern and if it's there, it's just imagination."

"It's a dangerous world these days," said Rhodes, as he got up, "and you know what they say about patterns: sometimes you only see the threads and not the big picture. I just stopped by to make sure you are not rushing into trouble here. I feel responsible."

They shook hands again.

"Promise me one thing, Carl," said Rhodes. "Or rather: two things."

The bizz jockey laughed. "I'll see what I can do."

"Bring your woman next time. She would love this place."

"If I bring her here, I'd better watch over her."

"A man should always watch over his woman."

"And the other thing?"

"You must promise to call me as soon as you run into difficulties here. You don't know this place. I do. Well. That's it then. I'm off again. Affairs of state to look into, Carl. See you soon, *amigo*."

Carl looked on as Colonel Rhodes walked briskly out of the VIP room.

What the hell was that all about, he wondered. Am I missing the big picture here?

Seven

Carl was starting to feel like a confused voter, who kept switching from left to right and back to left again, year after year.

Getting out of Caribal, the capital of Corazón, was basically limited to three options. The small airfield up on the Plato Grosso. The harbor. And third: the road that led up on the cliffs where the villas stood. There were simply no other ways, except for a few unpaved roads leading into the tropical rainforest that stretched in all directions. Although not an island, the Republic of Corazón lay isolated on the continent. The forest roads were used by forestry and mining corporations, and a few farmers, and those among them who were really drug traffickers, but seldom by anybody else. One could reach the border through the forest, but flying or sailing there was cheaper and faster. There were no trains in these parts.

A taxi drove Carl up the road leading to the top of the cliffs. It was nicely paved and wide and safe, but it was so full of hairpin turns that he almost got dizzy. There seemed no end to the taxi driver jerking the wheel. Left. Right. Left.

Right. Left. Right. First he thought of turning this into a nice one-liner about confused voters, but he abandoned that thought.

So he turned to the information Mach One had given him through the telephone earlier. The villa up there belonged to a man who went by the illustrious name of Auguste Fitzgeraldo.

"Sounds like a dictator to me," he had said.

There hadn't been much to tell about Fitzgeraldo other than that he was a spider in Corazón's financial world. His specialty seemed to be diverting money in and out of the country, out of sight of governments.

"He is entrusted with vast private wealth and apparently knows ways to go about in Corazón without ever getting into trouble," Mach One had said. "As far as I can see he keeps most of this money in Caribal's bank accounts, and probably a lot of it in gold in the vault."

"It can't be much of an international secret if you can dig this up so fast," Carl had said sarcastically.

"Don't bet on it. As usual you are underestimating my talent, Carl. But that's OK. If the governments of the USA, Europe and China find out what Fitzgeraldo is doing exactly, he's in deep trouble. I'll even bet that the junta of Corazón is unaware of this."

"Funny how your man, who is supposed to know all these secrets, ends up floating in the ocean beneath Auguste Fitzgeraldo's window," Carl had said.

To which Mach One's response had been short and swift. "I have underestimated the dangers of this assignment. This is no longer about evading taxes. This is no longer about the tax-free tropical paradise of Corazón. This is about criminals laundering money, hiding it from the world and keeping the actual owners of the money out of it. There are Beverly Hills top brass among them. Chinese top officials. British royalty. Be careful, Carl. Pry no further."

Carl laughed. *Pry no further.* The man had sounded like a character from a Sherlock Holmes novel. He was the Bizz Jockey, of all people! No one was going to stand in his way, because the world would know about it. He smelled a unique opportunity here.

Smelling opportunities requires certain talents. Carl Pappas certainly possessed some of these talents, but not all. The art of smelling opportunities is to go just far enough, but no further. Beyond a certain point, opportunities start to give off a stench.

It is in the smelling of these stenches that the true talent lies, the talent of the happy few.

The villa was hidden behind a three-meter high, white wall, with ivy growing over the top like a green waterfall. Carl went to the gate. Behind him the taxi drove back to Caribal.

Carl was allowed on the premises with surprising ease. A man in a dark suit, wearing impenetrable sunglasses, let him in, searched him for weapons and then escorted the bizz jockey across terraces and along a fountain around a corner to the front of the main house.

It was the house he'd seen from the *Rising Sun* all right. White, wide and with an immense wall of glass and a balcony across the entire length of the house. And, as suspected, a large swimming pool on a terrace larger than the building itself.

On the other side of the pool a man rose from a chair. There were other men, positioned at various corners of the house and the garden, hiding behind dark sunglasses. One held two Dobermans at a leash.

All of them, including the dogs, were looking at the arriving guest.

The man had walked towards Carl and stretched out a welcoming hand. "Allow me to introduce myself, Mr. Pappas. Auguste Fitzgeraldo, at your service."

"At my service?" asked Carl. He put up a grin and by doing so got rid of most of his nervousness at entering a lion's den.

Before him stood a man who did not meet his expectation after all that Mach One had told him. Even his name was out of proportion for this thin, muscular, quiet man. He did not smile, nor did he give Carl an unfavorable look. He simply kept his face neutral. He seemed unmoved by the bizz jockey's appearance. For Carl this was all acting; the man was obviously well prepared, how else could he have known the name of his guest?

"I like your dogs," said Carl. "I take it they attack at your command?"

Auguste Fitzgeraldo was dressed in a dark but brightly striped suit, wearing a blue shirt underneath. He seemed unaffected by the hot climate. Like the officials in this country he wore no sunglasses. His hair was greased and he sported a tiny mustache. He looked like a man in control. There was not a wrinkle in his face or in his suit. Carl had expected a man in his fifties, and that was about the only thing he got right. This was not the overfed godfather he had anticipated, the noisy chief of a gang of money launderers, this was a soft-spoken man with a weak handshake.

But the palm of his hand was as dry as the desert.

"Let's get right to the point, Mr. Pappas," said Fitzgeraldo after they were seated. "You don't mind if I do?"

Carl nodded. He watched a butler put down refreshments. The guards had disappeared from sight.

"I know who you are. I know the limelight you live in. I know that everything you touch and every man you meet ends up in that same limelight sooner or later. I, for one, do not like that limelight."

"Meaning?" said Carl.

"Meaning that I invite you to feel at home as long as you're my guest, but to forget about me the minute you walk out the gate."

"I can see what you're getting at," said Carl.

"Do you now?"

They both sipped from a bowl of tea.

Specialty of the house no doubt, thought Carl. This man wants to be of sound mind one hundred percent of the time. No room for alcohol in his plans.

"Yes. But you're making a mistake here. The times are changing, Mr. Fitzgeraldo. The current status quo in Corazón cannot be sustained."

"And what exactly has that to do with me?" Fitzgeraldo finally managed to add a little tone to his voice. It was the tone of disapproval. "Not everybody is susceptible to the influence of the bizz jockey, you know."

Carl put down his tea and sat back in a demonstrative way.

"Oh I'm just a pawn in the game of global economics. I have no influence."

"Come now, Mr. Pappas. You are being modest."

"No, really. I merely sail on the waves of change. Or on the winds, if you like. I focus the attention of my audience on stuff that is already happening."

"And what, would you say, is happening in Corazón?"

"I'd say the international community is about to put the limelight on the banks of Corazón and the origins of the money you have piled up there, Mr. Fitzgeraldo."

"I doubt that," said the tanned man with the mustache.

All of a sudden, out of the blue, the two Dobermans appeared around a corner of the house and ran towards them. They both positioned themselves at Carl's feet and sat there, their teeth blinking, their mouths slightly drooling. They looked up at him continuously.

"They're just being curious," said Fitzgeraldo. "Where was I. Oh yes, you implied I'm about to end up in your limelight. Are you threatening me, Mr. Pappas?"

"I am not in a position to threaten you," said Carl. He was quickly becoming uncomfortable with the dogs. "When was the last time they've eaten?"

"Like I said, they're just curious about our guests. I suppose my guard has released them for a while, allowed them to walk around freely. Do you want them... removed?"

They won't be the first who got removed today, thought Carl.

"No, I'm, fine. Really, I'm fine. Well, since you are a concise man, I guess I can be too. Here's my proposition. I will cancel my radio broadcast to my worldwide audience next Monday and forget about all the money that is hidden here in the vaults and bank accounts of Caribal."

Fitzgeraldo looked at his guest without moving a muscle in his face.

"If you persuade your clients to give away thirty percent of their assets in this country as a way of making good."

Fitzgeraldo choked on his tea. He engaged on a coughing fit so intense, he could have held a coughing game with Mach One. When he had calmed down, his face had lost its neutral expression altogether. "Making... making góód? What the hell is that supposed to mean?"

"Oh, you know what I mean. Making good for all the taxes they have evaded through the years."

"They don't have to pay any taxes here, for cryin' out loud!"

"I'm talking about the taxes they avoided paying in their home countries."

Auguste Fitzgeraldo tried to regain his neutral expression, but failed miserably. While wiping his face and his jacket with a handkerchief, he burst into laughter.

Laughter hollered over the pool, across the terrace and down the cliffs. He took his time laughing.

After a while Carl started to laugh as well.

Two of the security guys showed up to see what was going on, and then they started laughing too.

Finally the dogs started barking and the whole thing came to an abrupt end.

Auguste Fitzgeraldo stood up. He dried his eyes. "Enough of this chitchat. I expected the world's number one bizz jockey to do better. Well, it doesn't matter anymore now. By coming to Corazón you have already caused a stir. Thanks to you the ice has ruined the Martini. Regardless whether you broadcast on Monday or not, problems are already on their way."

Carl looked dumbfounded. For once, he found himself speechless at this sudden turn of the mood around him. The dogs had quieted simultaneously with the people here. Now three men and two dogs were once again staring at the bizz jockey, who was starting to feel lonely.

"So, señor bizz jockey, I invite you to witness my Plan B."

Eight

"Daddy's home," said Hitomi.

Her assistant looked up from her laptop, puzzled. She was a young girl who got paid a decent salary in spite of the fact that she was only an intern — on the insistence of the bizz jockey himself and much to the annoyance of boss Phil Solo. Employees of all kinds were treated well at WCBN Radio.

Hitomi pointed her face in the direction of the elevators. The Boardroom's sound engineer Don Wozniak was approaching.

"I didn't know Mr. Wozniak was married?" said the assistant.

"That's another matter. Can you imagine a woman, being of sound mind, wanting to get involved with that man?"

"No, I guess not."

"Exactly right," said Hitomi, right before Don arrived within hearing distance.

Now the girl was getting really confused. "Then why'd you say 'Daddy's home', Miss Sakamoto?"

Hitomi laughed, much to the surprise of the girl. "That's called cynicism, girl." Then she turned to her assistant, looked her over, but said nothing.

In her many years of working for The Boardroom, Hitomi had managed to pick up an international language, the language of witty ad libs, the way it had once been designed by American TV-sitcoms: never running out of steam, not necessarily relevant.

"Before any of you guys ask me where I've been, I'd like to make a statement," Don said. He was panting as if he had taken the stairs instead of the elevator.

"Don't bother, Don Lech Wozniak," said Hitomi. "Nobody is even remotely interested in your extracurricular activities in the capital of Corazón."

"I didn't feel like getting onboard the yacht of that, what's his name."

"Moon Afficionades."

"I think a man needs to rough it so I went into the nightlife right after our arrival."

"And you have your looks to prove it too. And your breath. At least you had the decency to take a shower," said Hitomi. Then she looked to her assistant and said: "Try not to think of him in the shower, OK?"

The girl burst out in laughter.

"Where's Carl?" said Don. "We were supposed to go through some of the technical stuff. The mikes, you know."

"No I don't," snarled Hitomi. "That's your department. Please leave us. We have stuff to do. But since you're up and running anyway, you might as well put some extra effort into finding Carl. I'm uncomfortable not knowing where he is. He's left the hotel, apparently, but left no messages."

"Tried his cell phone?"

"Not yet. Just get to him and do your mike thing, but make sure to confirm to me where you guys will be. Can you do that?"

"I'll get right on it, ma'am," said Don, winking to the assistant.

The girl just nodded back and Don walked off to the hotel terrace.

===

More than anything else, the terrace of the *Grand Corazón* was a timeless place. It offered a view of the Bay of Caribal that was unobstructed by modernities. No office buildings stood in the way, no electricity masts, no advertising billboards. In the distance, two to three kilometers away, the passage to the ocean allowed freighters and cruise ships to pass between the cliffs that marked the edges of the lagoon-shaped bay. On the water were many small sailing ships and a couple of yachts, but they all blended in nicely with the environment.

The terrace was built of a yellowish local stone and surrounded a large rectangular swimming pool that had been tiled in oceanic blue. Rows of palm trees stood along the sides, giving a nice shade to the many chairs made of tropical hardwood. On top of this, and hilarious to Don Wozniak, were the servants: they were all black men dressed meticulously in white uniforms, wearing white gloves. He wasn't sure what to think of it. The Republic of Corazón had a mixed population, with some Caribbean and Oriental influences floating on the surface, some Western blood and some African blood. Perhaps it was a remnant of the colonial time, Don thought.

He ordered a local drink called *Corabón*, pronounced with the emphasis on "bon", as in "good". He thought that was funny and wondered what it would taste like. But he also ordered two large cups of strong, black coffee, because he still had last night to deal with. The city center had been nice, but perhaps he had overdone it. Fortunately he had enough time to sober up before the live broadcast on Monday night.

After drinking one of the two cups of coffee he took off his Hawaiian printed shirt, looked at the lady next to him, a couple of chairs away, and answered her disapproving look with a wink. Then he got out his cell phone and called the bizz jockey's number. All he got was Carl Pappas' voicemail. So he left a short message.

"Yo, Carl, it's Don. You won't believe where I am: I'm sitting at the terrace at the *Grand Corazón*, I'm looking at the blue lagoon here, got coffee to get me back from Mars and I am now going to enhance my life by trying the local specialty called 'Corabon'. That's Cora-BON. Get it? Bon? Listen, call me when you're ready to check out the tech. Any time's fine for me."

Then he put the cell phone away and looked ahead. For a moment Don Wozniak marveled at the view, and how the other city buildings were hidden from view by rows of palm trees on the left and the right. He knew there was a road between the hotel and the beach, but it was one story lower than the terrace, so it was entirely overlooked.

Let's do it, Don thought.

He lifted the drink, a tall, thin glass with a slice of pineapple attached to the top. He smelled it. It gave off wonderful aromas of coconut and vanilla and cinnamon.

The moment Don Wozniak lifted the glass to his mouth, at 4 p.m. plus a few minutes, time seemed to come to a halt. First he saw a blinding light flash, which caused him to sit up straight and spill some of his *Corabón*. Then his ears were hit with the full force of a large explosion. Finally a shockwave shook the trees, caused the pool water to jump up a bit, and rumbled the terrace floor.

By that time Don found out he was only holding the remains of glass in his fist. He had crushed his much-anticipated *Corabón*.

"Not so 'bon'," he mumbled, in shock.

Nine

Smoke and ashes were raining down on the terrace. Someone shook Don's shoulder and he looked Hitomi Sakamoto right in the eye.

"You... you OK, Wozniak-san?" said Hitomi.

For a change she looked genuinely worried. The woman bent over and started wiping dust off Don's face. Then she stood back and looked at the mess.

"A building has just exploded," she said. "They say it's a local bank."

"Far out!" yelled Don, getting up. "Ouch!"

He had gripped the chair with a hand full of glass.

"You stupid man," shouted Hitomi, upset. "You are coming with me nów to the first aid... eh... person in the hotel."

She grabbed Don's other hand and dragged him away from the scene, into the hotel.

"You been able to reach Carl in the mean time?" said Hitomi.

"Nope. Got his voicemail."

"This is ridiculous. What if he went to talk to one of the bankers here? There's something going on and I don't like it.

After we fix your hand we're going to take action."

"Duh... and do what? In countries like this they blow up buildings all the time. Probably just a car bomb," protested Don. "Ouch!"

"That's in the Middle East. Not here. This is actually one of the quietest countries you can go to. No homicides in the past twelve months, did you know that? I thought we did the right thing coming here, but now I'm beginning to doubt it."

They arrived at the main desk in the lobby. Outside, a tsunami of sirens, from police cars and fire trucks and ambulances, had broken out. From the elevators and stairways came an outpour of worried guests.

Hitomi made her way through the crowd and, miraculously, got the attention of one of the receptionists immediately. "This man has been wounded," she barked across the counter. "He's in pain, you need to do something nów."

While Don was escorted into an adjoining staff room, Hitomi looked through the crowd and spotted a familiar face. "Colonel!" she shouted.

Towering in the crowd was the figure of Colonel Rhodes, accompanied by some men in military uniforms. He made a few gestures and the men created a passage towards the reception.

"Miss Sakamoto, I am very glad to see you. I have been trying to reach Mr. Pappas but I have been unable to find him. This is most unfortunate," said Rhodes, while making a courteous bow and shaking Hitomi's hand.

"Unfortunate? Why?"

"We have yet to fully ascertain the situation. In a few moments I'll be briefed by my colleague, the Minister of

Security. He is on the spot. But I decided to make a stop here first, see if my *amigo* Mr. Pappas is alright. You don't know where he is?"

"No. Although that doesn't have to mean anything... Unless..." Hitomi hesitated. "Do you think the explosion at the bank is an accident?"

The Colonel smiled. "My dear Miss Sakamoto. Money may have its explosive traits in an economic way of speaking, but it never blows up in real life. No, this is the result of a very, very large bomb."

He shook her hand again. "I have to go now. But I will be back within half an hour. If Mr. Pappas has not shown up, I will personally lead an official search for him. Is that satisfactory for you, milady?"

The producer touched her hair for a moment. "Well... Thank you very much, Colonel, you are hitting the nail on the head."

"Miss Sakamoto," said the Colonel. He made a short bow, more like a jerk of his upper torso, and walked away, the soldiers in his slipstream, the crowd suddenly opening up to give passage to an important man.

===

A green light penetrating the eyelids. Hundreds of small dots rushing through it. Rumbling in the ears. A pain in the neck. The slow realization of movement, then the full awareness of being shaken, hard and rough. The smell of a Cuban cigar.

With a pang, Carl opened his eyes.

Everything he had come to suspect while slowly returning

to consciousness, appeared correct. He was sitting in a jeep. The jeep was moving fast, across an unpaved road, through a tropical rainforest. The jungle canopy turned the remaining rays of the late afternoon sun into a greenish light. The millions of leaves threw additional dot-like shadows in the mix. The ride was bumpy.

The bizz jockey was sitting on the back seat. The front seats were occupied by two men. He could not see them clearly yet.

"Why am I here," said Carl, as loud as he could with the force he could muster; which wasn't much.

The face of Auguste Fitzgeraldo came around the front seat. The man behind the wheel also turned, and Carl recognized one of Fitzgeraldo's well-dressed thugs.

"Why, señor Pappas, glad to have you back," said Fitzgeraldo.

"Who hit me?"

"One of my men, I'm afraid."

"Whó hit me?"

"That would be Joaquín, I'm sorry to say. But don't be too hard on him, he was only acting on my orders."

Fitzgeraldo's hand appeared, holding the cigar Carl had smelled, and put it in his owner's mouth. The man took a draw and blew it towards the open window. "As a man of business, Mr. Pappas, you will appreciate the notion of rules. Business works only if we all abide to certain rules. If one party decides to ignore the rules, it usually costs the other party a lot of money."

While his host was talking, Carl noticed at least he wasn't tied or anything. He just had a nasty bump on the back of his head.

"In your case that is probably an incredible amount of money that isn't even your own," said Carl. He looked through the front window and saw a truck, and then, as the road turned a little bit, he saw more trucks in front of it. The trucks were closed and revealed nothing of their cargo. "Don't tell me... You've got to be kidding. You put the money in these trucks?"

"Gold," said Fitzgeraldo. "I'm shipping out. I need to protect the assets of my clients. No thanks to you, I might add."

The bizz jockey moved to sit upright. Then he heard a loud noise, something resembling an explosion in the distance, something that made him turn and look through the rear window. Only the tiniest stripe of blue sky was visible above the trees, and through it a huge bolt of fire and smoke could be seen clearly, rising up into the sky. The rumbling faded quickly.

"You are nuts," said Carl. "Let me guess: you blew up the bank. You drive off with the gold. You think no one's gonna know?"

"No I do not think that," growled Fitzgeraldo in a whirl of cigar smoke. "It is of no consequence. We will bring the gold across the border, where I will hide it till the storm blows over. With no gold ánd, please pay attention here, no bank accounts left, there will be no one to blame. Not a single name. Who are they going to turn to? My clients? All information has been destroyed. So you've sent a hacker punk to break into the bank of Corazón, Mr. Pappas. Well, there's nothing left to hack now, is there?"

The next puff of cigar smoke was aimed right at Carl's face. He coughed. It took a while.

Then Carl caught his breath again and he asked: "What hacker punk?"

"Don't play innocent with me, señor Bizz Jockey. You know who I mean. I know you sent that man. Well, I persuaded him to resign his hacking assignment and enjoy the good life of Corazón. Wanted to do some diving off the cliffs under my terrace. A man with a knack for adventure, wouldn't you say?"

It was not a question Carl felt inclined to answer. He remained silent, brooding over the whole situation. A more important question needed to be answered, but he didn't feel like asking it: why had Fitzgeraldo brought the bizz jockey along on his flight?

"I know what you're thinking, señor. You are not tied. You can jump out of the car. Well, we'll just stop this jeep and shoot you. You are coming along until we have reached the border of Corazón. You are my guarantee for safe passage. I assure you this government is not going to bomb a caravan of gold when the world's most famous radio host is on it."

The man laughed again, so loud that the driver joined in.

It reminded Carl of the two Dobermans, who had interrupted Fitzgerald's last outburst.

"Didn't bring your dogs, Fitzgerald?"

"No. They're taking the scenic route."

Then Fitzgeraldo returned to a normal position in his seat and started talking into a large satellite phone.

Ten

The white villa on top of the cliffs was definitely abandoned. The main gate was open and the doors were unlocked.

Hitomi and Don had left the taxi waiting outside the white wall. After doing some inquiries they'd found the driver through the hotel reception; the driver who had brought the bizz jockey to this house earlier that day. They had walked across the path to the terrace and the swimming pool, yelling "Hello?" and "Anybody home?" Don had even yelled "We're lost!" in an attempt to provide themselves with an alibi, but Hitomi had kicked him.

"Shut up, Wozniak, you'll only make us look more suspicious. This place is not big enough to get lost."

From the terrace they could see the bay, deep below. Further in the distance, an enormous black cloud of smoke rose from the city of Caribal.

"This is ridiculous," said Hitomi. "Carl goes up here for a visit, and the whole place turns out to be abandoned. The city's on fire by now. What is going on? If Phil Solo hears about this he's going to bring in an army to get Carl out on the double, and then fire me."

They were alarmed by the sounds of roaring engines, squeaking tires and doors slamming.

"That'll be the Colonel," said Hitomi and she was right.

"You are a courageous woman, Miss Sakamoto," said Colonel Rhodes as he approached, accompanied by two soldiers. He had changed into a military combat outfit. "But you are also taking too much risk. Why didn't you wait until I arrived with my team? I was only two minutes behind you. What if there had been armed men here?"

"The gate was open wide, there were no cars," said Hitomi in a decisive tone.

"That makes sense. Listen, I got the information, this house was inhabited by señor Fitzgeraldo, a shady character if you ask me. A financial man, a middle man who moves money across the globe."

"Dangerous man?" asked Don.

"I've seen him a couple of times, he's got several contacts at government level. Always in the company of bodyguards, you know, the kind that give ordinary folk the creeps. Black suits, sunglasses, dogs. Other than that, I wouldn't know."

A cell phone rang and the Colonel turned away to answer it. After a while he turned to Hitomi and Don again. "I think I know where señor Pappas is, and señor Fitzgeraldo. I would like to invite you to come along, Miss Sakamoto. You seem suited for combat situations."

"Well... Hey, what about me?" yelled Don. He started to follow the troupe back to the gate. "Where is Carl, you say?"

"I just got the word on what happened at the bank downtown," said Colonel Rhodes. "It turns out the contents of the bank have been taken in trucks, in the direction of the

Plato Grosso. All account information has been destroyed as well. That means a large amount of gold is being shipped out illegally right now. We are going in pursuit."

"Awesome!" said Don. "Exciting place. But you've still not told us where Carl Pappas is."

"He's with them," said Hitomi. "Isn't that obvious? I'm with you, Colonel."

They mounted one of the army vehicles and before Don could interfere, all four cars drove off in a cloud of dust.

Don walked over to the taxi and got in. "I told Carl to not get involved in local politics, just enjoy the time here and do a good show and kick some ass on the radio, but remember all the time that this is a police state. So what happens? A war breaks out. Rockin'!"

The taxi driver was looking at him dumbfounded.

"The *Grand Corazón*," said Don. "But I suppose you've already guessed that. I mean, where else can you go in this banana republic?"

"Bananas," said the taxi driver cheerfully. "You like? Very good, eh, our bananas? Best in the world. Just a poco expensive, no?"

===

Alejandro Bolas, the fire chief of Caribal, was not happy this evening. The fire that had started as a mere side effect of the explosion at the central bank of Corazón earlier in the afternoon had moved up in the list of priorities. By the time the sun set over the Republic, all casualties had been taken care of and it had been established there was no further danger of collapsing walls or residual explosions. But the fire had spread across a couple of buildings and found a way to the trees. It was the dry season. A tropical rainforest is less likely to burn than a normal forest, but it can burn nevertheless. What they were facing now was a hopeless situation.

The wind blew inland from the ocean, goading the fire to eat right into the jungle, up to the Plato Grosso and into all mainland directions. There weren't even enough roads to get everywhere, if they had the fire trucks to do it. Which they didn't either.

An hour after sundown Bolas' team had secured the city. Six buildings had burned down, but there had been no casualties there and the fire was now completely under control. But in the distance, it raged on.

Right when he was about to issue new orders, a military jeep pulled up next to him. One of the military junta members, Colonel Rhodes, jumped out.

"Chief?"

"Your excellency?"

"Skip the formalities, chief. I need your help. A caravan of trucks has left the city. I have ordered the army to pursue them."

"That's going to be difficult. They are on the other side of the fire. Before morning comes it will be the greatest forest fire this continent has ever seen. Unfortunately I do not have the resources to stop it."

The Colonel shook his head impatiently. "Not stop. Just create a passage for us to follow them. That'll do."

"I doubt if that's possible, sir. Why not send helicopters?"

"And do what? Shoot rockets at trucks full of gold? No, this is a ground war. Let's go chief, on the double."

Chief Bolas gestured the Colonel to mount the first fire truck. "Wait here for a moment," he said, "while I instruct the other men."

Inside the truck, the fireman behind the wheel was bent over a map. The Colonel joined him. Close to the bank building a road went straight inland and up the Plato Grosso. From there on it was thousands of kilometers to the border of Corazón, a line waving and bending like a river.

"I've driven that road many times before, when I was a truck driver, excellency," said the fireman. "It can be done, but there are always many unscheduled stops."

"Why?"

"A tree blocking the road. A sudden hole after heavy rainfall. The crossing of a river."

"Surely there are bridges in Corazón?"

"Some crossings are bridges, excellency."

"Well, fireman, you better be prepared to ride up front. You know the road and you know the fire. We have some rescuing to do. A lot of gold and one soul."

===

Bopac Obrador was returning from a herb hunt, deep in the forests on the Plato Grosso. It would take him less than two hours on foot now, to reach the city. He followed an old native trail that was too narrow for cars. That way he didn't have to worry about huge trucks suddenly appearing out of nowhere in the darkness. The official road that led across the high plateau to the border was a dangerous road that he never took.

The tropical rainforest was a goldmine for his small herb shipping business. Clients from all over the world ordered exotic herbs through his website and he'd collect them himself. It made enough money to live a wealthy life and all the herb shipping was perfectly legal. Mainly leaves of strong tropical trees and plants, pieces of bark, bundles of grass.

His trip had been good. But about half an hour ago he had started to smell something funny. At first he had no idea what it was. But after a while he recognized it. There was a fire.

He had not smelled this in a long time. Fires were rare in Corazón, at least in his lifetime so far. So naturally it worried him. Where was the fire? Was it in the city? In the forest? Down here between the trees, far below the forest canopy, it was hard to tell which way the wind was blowing. Even when the smoke started to become visible, there was still no trace of a draft that told him from which way the smoke was coming.

This pissed him off to no end. He absolutely needed to know the direction of the fire or he would have no idea in which direction to proceed. One doesn't want to walk right into a fire.

Forty-five minutes after he first noticed the smell, the smoke began to thicken rapidly. It was becoming unbearable. Bopac took a cloth out of his backpack and tied it around his head, covering his nose and mouth. But by then his eyes had started to water.

"Time to go," he mumbled.

With the backpack full of herbs he started to climb one of

the giant tropical trees. He picked one that was thick enough to put your arms and legs around, and rough enough to prevent him from sliding. In Caribal, children learn to climb the trees at a young age, and Bopac had been no exception. Unlike most people, he had also maintained his tree climbing skills for the benefit of reaping the jungle's herb harvests. So quick as a monkey he moved up the tree, for dozens of meters, until he reached the canopy. After some additional climbing he could stick his head beyond the leaves and look around, over the jungle.

In the early dark of the night most of the black smoke eluded him, but that didn't matter. A wall of flames rose above the forest. To Bopac's horror, it looked as if all these flames suddenly turned their ugly heads and looked straight at him.

There were less than fifty meters between him and the fire.

Eleven

"What the hell's the matter with you?" snarled Auguste Fitzgeraldo. "You OK? You're sweating like a maniac."

"Oh, I'm feeling a little nauseous, sir," said the jeep driver. He wiped his hands dry on his pants, one by one, but that didn't seem to help. The wheel was already soaked.

"Nauseous my ass," said Carl. "That man has a sudden attack of a tropical disease."

"Are you an expert in tropical diseases, Sir?" said the driver.

"Oh shut up, of course he's not. Maybe it's a passing thing," said Fitzgeraldo. "And if it's not we'll deal with it later. We will be making several stops and the first one's right ahead."

The night was pitch black. If it was a moonlight night, there was no way to tell down here. The trees had created a perfect roof that kept the road sealed off from the sky almost all the way. In front of them were the red taillights of a truck, too far for the headlights of their jeep.

Fitzgeraldo dialed his satellite phone.

"Issue an order for all trucks to switch off all lights befóre we get to the first Caramazon crossing. Get that? Great. Then listen good. It is absolutely essential that every vehicle is proceeded by a walking man. You hear me? There must be eye contact between each walking man and truck driver. They can use small flashlights if necessary. We do not want the trucks to bump into each other or run into some kind of obstacle. The whole caravan must stop before the bridge. No one crosses before I give the word."

He put the phone away into his large overcoat.

"Quite an undertaking," said Carl. "Are you expecting an attack from the air?"

"Not really. Corazón doesn't have a squad ready with men who can parasail down in the middle of the night and raid us. That happens only in the movies, or perhaps the Americans do it. But not here. On the other hand, why take unnecessary risks?"

Fifteen minutes later the caravan had come to a halt. The jeep was last in line.

"Listen," said Fitzgeraldo, "I'm going to the front of the line to make sure they cross the river in an orderly fashion. This bridge is straight out of *Bridge On The River Kwai* and we need to be extra careful. Do not move or do anything until I get back."

He got out of the car, but before he closed the door he added: "And switch off your lights."

Then he walked off and it was dark.

A little while later Carl's eyes were getting used to the dark and he started to see parts of the surroundings. Not the jungle right beside the car; there it remained pitch black. By hanging out the window he could look beyond the truck in front of them and see a clearing in the forest. A moon shone down and there were contours of an enormous bridge. It was a complex construction of wood, but it was hard to see any details. Judging from the sound of it, the trucks up front were moving again.

"A night of adventure," said Carl.

There was no reply from the driver.

"Imagine I could have been sitting on the terrace of the *Grand Corazón* right now and having a drink with my team mates."

Still no reply.

Carl bent forward and took a look. The driver was either sleeping or unconscious. His forehead was wet like a swimmer's.

"You áre ill," said Carl, a little bit louder. "Admit it!"

No reply. There was no time to waste. He tried one of the doors — it was open.

Unfortunately, before he could push it open further, the truck before them started the engine again and started to move, Auguste Fitzgeraldo suddenly popped up out of nowhere and the driver woke up.

Auguste opened the door and said: "I'll walk you across. Stay close so you can see me. If you are in doubt, stop the car immediately. Whatever you do, do not switch on the lights."

He slammed the door shut and disappeared in front of the jeep. Only his silhouette could now be seen. As the truck in front of them moved away and the jeep started to drive forward very slowly, the moon got a chance to light up the spot. The large carcass of the wooden bridge hovered above them like an installation in an amusement park. Any moment now, Carl expected the carts of a roller-coaster to come roaring down. And up again.

But there was no movement other than that of the silhouette of Fitzgeraldo, and the sound of the jeeps' engine.

But still, there was a chance for the bizz jockey. Just a few meters...

===

Seated in the jungle canopy, Bopac Obrador felt the beginning of panic. The fire was very close now. Climbing down was no longer an option. The thick fog of smoke would render him unconscious within minutes. Escaping on the ground was a thing of the past. He now tried to establish the precise direction of the fire. What if it moved in a different direction and passed him by?

That's wishful thinking, Obrador, he thought. You fool.

He started moving across the branches, from one tree to another. The height was frightening, although the darkness was now complete. It was a starry, moonlit night, and that helped a bit. But he knew he was not making enough progress. A fire like this might travel with the speed of a runner, say eight kilometers an hour. Of course it could also be four, or sixteen, hard to tell. But the fire would always outrun him. He felt like a clumsy candidate for a monkey's exam.

There may be a price to pay, Obrador, he thought. And no herbs are going to save your life if it comes to that!

===

The jeep drove slowly onto the wooden bridge. The whole construction was shrouded in darkness and looked like it was painted black. Through the wooden beams Carl could see the stars. The truck in front of them was no longer visible. He could not even see Auguste Fitzgeraldo.

So much the better, Carl thought. It must be done now and it must be done fast.

He opened the door without a sound, stepped out of the car and reached the right side of the bridge. The best thing to do now, he had decided, was to jump in the river. It would be the fastest way of quickly putting a safe distance between him and his captors. They would be unable to shoot him in the darkness. No one would jump after him, they would have to climb down to the riverbed and by that time he would have swam away. In addition to that, the river was also a convenient way for him to navigate out of this place. Running into the bushes was not going to be very helpful, he would primarily get lost.

So he climbed over the beam and looked down.

And froze.

The river was so far beneath him that he could not properly determine the distance. Nor could he see if the water was deep enough for a dive, or if there were any obstacles. The moon shone on the water, he could see the river surface properly, but he was afraid to jump.

"Come now, señor Carl. Don't tell me you haven't the guts. So far you've impressed me, but now I'm beginning to doubt."

Carl looked behind him and saw Auguste Fitzgeraldo lighting a cigar. In the flickering light he spotted two of his bodyguards.

"Go ahead. Jump. I promise you my men won't shoot you."

Carl looked down again.

"They won't have to, because you would not survive such a jump. Now if you please, follow us to the car and…"

A roaring sound interrupted Fitzgeraldo. It was the sound of an approaching fighter.

"Damn!" shouted Fitzgeraldo. He held a hand over his cigar. "Come off that edge, Pappas, and don't make a sound. I have more to lose than you."

Carl was grabbed and jerked off the beam. He was carried to the center of the bridge. A gun was placed at his temple.

"Be very quiet, Mr. Pappas."

"Like a jet fighter is going to hear me shout. Are you stupid?"

The fighter roared overhead with enormous speed, followed by a second plane. Within seconds, the air was cleared and it was quiet again.

"OK let's move it. Get him to the car and tie him up. We need to speed things up a bit."

While they moved, the moon disappeared behind a cloud.

Twelve

The Plato Grosso stretched into the continent like an ink spot on the globe, vast and uninterrupted. It lifted the soil to an approximate altitude of twelve-hundred meters above sea level and was covered by a tropical rainforest. Although it was not limited to one country alone, Corazón was the only nation that was almost entirely swallowed by the Grosso. The plateau left but a small stretch of lower land to the people of the Republic, around the bay of Caribal.

The firm stance of the military junta of Corazón had kept farmers and businesses from burning down large chunks of the forest, as had been a habit in most other countries who were lucky enough to possess such natural resources. Any attempt at taking down trees other than sustainable forestry had been met with military retribution. But that was all in the past; no one dared enter the area with a chainsaw these days. The uninhabited, tree-infested territory of Corazón was immense and allowed tree-cutting to go undetected for quite a while, but the penalties were too high. Some people who had been at work in the jungle without the proper permits two decades ago were still imprisoned, and the junta made sure everybody heard about it regularly.

The downside of this approach was of course that the Plato Grosso was mainly an undiscovered country, with only a few unpaved roads that led nowhere, and, in the end, only two roads that led more or less directly to the border. One of them followed the coastline.

The other road, moving into the continent almost in a straight line, was getting crowded. From her seat in the front of the army jeep, sitting between a soldier behind the wheel on her left and Colonel Rhodes on her right, Hitomi saw a line of army vehicles standing completely still. The line of cars and trucks stretched on behind them.

A couple of army guys, all with firm mustaches and stars and stripes on their camouflage army uniforms, stood by the car window on the Colonel's side. They were lit by flashlights, held by a couple of soldiers. They were discussing options and it all proceeded with such ease and determination, hardly without argument, that Hitomi's thoughts had wondered off to another world for a moment.

Why is it, she thought, that a team meeting of The Boardroom looks more like a war than a team meeting of the Corazón military junta staff? Here's a crisis and they are all talking in the calmest, controlled and cooperative manner imaginable. None of the sarcasm and shouting abuse that is so common at WCBN Radio.

"Why can't we move forward?" asked Hitomi, when the Colonel turned to her again.

"The fire is moving too slow," he answered. "The forest fire is moving right in front of us, away from us. It's following the precise trajectory of this road."

"Well," said Hitomi impatiently, "get around it!"

Rhodes smiled. "My dear Miss Sakamoto, there is no way around it. Around this road are thousands of kilometers of tropical rainforest. We are stuck here."

The producer sighed and put a hand on the Colonel's arm. "Colonel-san. Can't you send in some choppers? Can't you send in a team that jumps from a plane right on top of them and liberates Carl Pappas? His life is in danger, you see." She added a smile. "I'm sure you have the power to fix this."

"We have no such team, Miss Sakamoto. There is no place to land a helicopter for at least three-hundred kilometers. It is also dark."

He took her hand.

This is not going anywhere, Hitomi thought.

"Can't you move in from the other side?"

"The... other side? You mean, from the other side of the Plato Grosso? That would mean involving one of our neighbors and that is, I regret to say, not an option."

Hitomi squeezed the hand. "And why's that?"

"Let's not get into politics, Miss Sakamoto," said the Colonel, putting his other hand on top of Hitomi's. Now he held her with both hands. He thought of saying something in the line of "why don't we talk about something else while waiting," but Hitomi's hand disappeared from his grip.

"That's simply nót satisfactory, Colonel Rhodes," she hissed.

"I see your point," said Rhodes. He was not a man who was easily taken aback. "I suggest you and I light a cigar and discuss our options. You are a vigilant young lady. I will listen to any suggestion you are willing to offer me."

"That's all very well," said Hitomi, smiling. "But the driver gets a cigar too. Team building, you know."

"I love team building," said the Colonel, getting his cigar box. "And how about you?"

"You need to get on the phone, Colonel," said Hitomi, accepting a cigar. "You need to get the weather forecast."

===

Bopac Obrador sat high in the night. He stared at the skies. Behind him the light radiated by the forest fire grew stronger. So far he had been lucky; all smoke from the fire had fallen down to the ground and passed underneath him. Up here, dozens of meters above the ground, he could still smell the freshness of the tropical natural richness, albeit mixed with the smell of fire. He had already chosen a way of dying and it had to be grand. No point in climbing down and getting suffocated by the smoke and falling flat unconscious. That was truly a grey death. No, he had decided to just wait till the fire reached the giant tree he was sitting on and then fly to his death like an angel lit from within. It suited his belief in a world beyond death, in an unknown paradise, a reincarnation perhaps. He sat there imagining his last flight, a slow descent into the heat, lights all around him, voices encouraging him in the blaze of fire. A homecoming. He started to say a prayer.

The strong light from the fire and the dream he was dreaming and the prayer he was saying prevented him from paying any attention to the wind that had been growing stronger and stronger in the past hour, and the cloud front that had been crawling across the ocean and was now starting to hover over him. In a few moments, the moon would disappear for a long time to come.

Thirteen

The truck in front of them was moving so fast, its red tail lights were beginning to disappear in a fog of sand and dust, brightly lit by the headlights of Auguste Fitzgeraldo's car.

"Step on it, man," complained Auguste. "We need to stay right on their tail."

The car hit a hole, made a downward movement on the driver's side and then jumped up.

The driver cursed, and his voice was full of pain.

Now Fitzgeraldo cursed too and grabbed the wheel with his left hand. "Stop the freakin' car, man! STOP IT NOW! Hit the brakes…"

With a croaking sound and with sand whirling around them, the car came to a stop. The driver leaned over the wheel.

"I think he passed out," said Carl. His hands were tied to his back and the jump the car had made had launched him against the roof, and then sideways against the window. There was no way he could touch any of the new bruises on his head.

"I can see that," said Fitzgeraldo. He reached for his

satellite phone and engaged in a short conversation. "Stop the caravan," he said. "My driver's sick, he needs to be replaced right now. Send a couple of guys back here, we're a couple of hundred meters behind, that's my estimate."

He threw the phone on the dashboard and stepped out. Then he sniffed.

"There's a fire," he said to Carl, through the open door. "It can't be the bank's explosion, we're too far away now. It must be a forest fire."

He reached for the phone again, saying "I need to know what's going on there."

Once the number was dialed, he talked, much quieter than before. Carl could still hear it, but obviously Fitzgeraldo was making some kind of clandestine call.

"What's happening in the city, Jorge... Whát? A forest fire? ... It's blocking their way... How convenient... If they move again, call me."

Standing next to the car, Fitzgeraldo looked up towards the sky, but it was pitch black. The jungle canopy probably covered the road from the heavens, but it was hard to tell.

Three men appeared into the car's headlights. They were trained security men, who didn't need to talk before commencing with their task. Two of them removed the limp body of the driver and carried him back to where they came from, disappearing into the darkness almost as swift as they had arrived. The third man took the wheel. By that time Fitzgeraldo had stepped back into the car, so the new driver drove off immediately.

From the back seat, Carl noticed how Fitzgeraldo was wiping his forehead with a handkerchief.

===

The flames were reaching for him. But they were no longer scaring Bopac. By now, they were the arms of angels coming to his rescue. It was hard to tell whether it was the high concentration of oxygen, which is typical for a rainforest, or the anxiety that had caused him to hallucinate, but it was effective nonetheless. The small man with his boney and leathery face, worn out by so many years of travelling outside in the jungle and on his small fishing boat, had turned around to face the fire. He saw the faces and wings of angels rising above the forest roof, moving around wildly like in some elaborate dance ritual. And he thought he heard music, some Spanish fandango perhaps, or a pavane, from slow to frantic to slow again, and all this came closer and closer, and now they were stretching their heavenly arms... They were reaching out for him. Bopac stretched his arm and reached back to them...

His body started to tingle. First he felt it in his bare forearms. A tingling sensation on the skin of his hands and his arms. It started tiny, but then all of a sudden it gained strength and then it was all over him and he started to feel it on his head and his face and...

My dear Lord, thought Bopac Obrador, listen, listen, they are screaming, they are in pain, dear Lord, what is happening to your angels?

The rain came now with full force, pouring down on the Plato Grosso as if a switch was turned somewhere. It would be scientifically impossible to have more water fall down simultaneously than at this very moment.

As a result, Bopac woke from his hallucination with a shock, almost losing his balance, high on the trees. He grabbed the branch and laid his body flat on it, and wrapped his legs around it for support. He needed all his powers to resist the downpour and prevent a deadly fall.

As soon as he felt in control again, he started to climb down. He had to get down, get out of this place, and he had to get out as fast as he could. He decided that if he made it down and the fire had indeed been tamed by the rain, he would get to the road and hitchhike back with any vehicle that came his way.

He never looked back at the dying angels.

===

Finally they were moving again. Hitomi sat on the front seat and tried to hold on to something. That proved to be a difficult task, because the jeep had no seat belts. There was nothing to hold onto on the dashboard but the wheel. So every time there was a bump in the road and they were all launched, Hitomi had to grab Colonel Rhodes' arm or leg; though usually he had already grabbed her instead. She was growing a bit tired of all this. But it was a minor disadvantage she was willing to endure for the sake of the safe return of the bizz jockey. Moving forward was now the most important thing.

And moving forward they were. The speed of the army caravan had been prepped up to irresponsible limits. They were literally blazing through the forest. The rain had been pouring for fifteen minutes now, as if heaven sent. The water had dealt with the fire, but the vision was poor and there was the danger of slipping.

"Any chance of running into oncoming cars?" shouted Hitomi.

The noise the car made was something to take into account.

"Night traffic is low in these parts," shouted Rhodes. "Possibly one truck per hour. But word has been spread there's a forest fire and there's an army pursuit going on, so I doubt if any truck will continue its journey. They'll stop at one of the villages along..."

"Watch that bend," shouted Hitomi to the driver. She was one step away from kicking him out and taking the wheel herself. Rescuing the bizz jockey was one thing, but she wouldn't be able to make a difference if she ended up in a tropical car crash.

The headlights were partially dimmed by the rain, and whatever was around the bend was not going to be revealed until the very last moment.

That proved to be too late.

A shadow moved in front of the lights. Everybody opened his mouth to shout something, but it had already happened: the army jeep drove into Bopac Obrador with such force, that he was jerked to the side, run over by one wheel. The second wheel projected him into the bushes that he had emerged from.

The jeep slid sideways into the side of the road, a black mass of leaves, but fortunately not the solid mass of a tree trunk. The leaves softened the speed and the car came to a halt.

Hitomi had been rescued from slamming into the dashboard by the firm grip of Colonel Rhodes.

"You can let go now, Colonel."

It took him a moment. After that he looked embarrassed. His grip had been... tight.

"Mán...," moaned Hitomi. "You saved my life."

That was, as far as the producer was concerned, an unprecedented event.

Before Colonel Rhodes could respond, the driver looked at Hitomi with a big smile. "Anything for the señora."

"It was probably some animal," yelled the Colonel. "Back up this vehicle, soldier. We have no time to loose with chitchat. We're way behind."

===

Bopac Obrador lay underneath the bushes on the forest floor. He was surrounded by a complete darkness and there was nothing above him but branches and leaves, hiding him from the sky. But once more, the dying angels came to him in his final, blurry vision. He knew now that they had not given up and were coming to rescue him after all.

Fourteen

It would be easier to fly to the moon and drive the first Lunar Roving Vehicle — forever parked on the bleak surface of the earth's only satellite — around the dust than to get this party moving again.

Two trucks carrying Auguste Fitzgeraldo's clients' fortunes were stranded in the mud of the road and they were going to remain there for quite a while. Half an hour earlier the caravan had come to a halt in one of the very few junctions in the forest. From here, trekker paths led in several directions. The main road split in two more unpaved roads, that by now had turned into muddy affairs and were beginning to resemble small rivers. They had stopped here to deal with one problem, and then found themselves facing two.

Auguste's sick driver's condition had deteriorated so fast that they no longer dared transport him in a truck jumping up and down in the mud. They had moved him to a small, abandoned building that stood exactly in the V of the two main roads. It was unlocked and served as an emergency post for all traffic across the Plato Grosso. There was some open space to park cars and trucks, a medical aid supply and a pump that brought up fresh water from deep below. There were also a few bunks. They had put the driver on one of the bunks and then he had died.

Frantic consultation took place in and around Fitzgeraldo's car, so Carl was able to follow the proceedings quite closely.

"First the good news," said one of Fitzgeraldo's men, a hulk of a guy with large whiskers and a camouflage outfit, which could mean he was a member of the army, but it was probably just a private outfit of a man eager to make a fashion statement. He was armed with two automatic weapons, hanging around his neck. "By accident we have stopped exactly at a junction. That gives us the option to have a helicopter land here. The bad news is that two of the trucks have sunk into the mud while we were standing still. Getting them out is going to be impossible without equipment, which we don't have right now. They are also blocking the way out for the other trucks. The road to the left takes us too far and towards the wrong border. We have to take the road on the right and now we can't."

"I take it," said Fitzgeraldo grimly, "that everybody has already heard the other bad news: the army is in pursuit and their path is no longer blocked by the forest fire."

The man in the camouflage suit spoke again. "We are outrunning them by several hours. My estimate is they'll be here in four hours. Now that we're standing still, they will be gaining on us of course. We'll regroup indoors to look at the map and organize our next move. Move it people, we are running out of time."

"And luck," said Carl.

They all looked in his direction.

Then, as the group dispersed, Fitzgeraldo said to Carl: "No we're not. And you know what: neither are you. You take part in the greatest heist in history, well it's not a heist really, but I'm not sure what to call it. You get to be part of a great adventure. Isn't that a lot more exciting than a radio show?"

"Whatever," said Carl. "But I'd appreciate it if you had my hands untied. This stuff really hurts. And this way I cannot even defend myself against a spider."

"Sure. I mean, where would you like to run, my dear bizz jockey?" said Fitzgerald, as he wiped his forehead.

"Is that the same fever that just killed your driver?" said Carl, while his hands were being released from their ties.

Fitzgeraldo did not respond. He pulled his guest out of the car and walked him to the building that stood hiding under the trees. The rain still poured down relentlessly.

Inside, the man in the camouflage suit was bent over a table, surrounded by at least a dozen other men. There was a portable gas lamp on the table. Carl presumed they were looking at a map. He was pushed to a chair and seated, while Fitzgeraldo put the satellite phone to his ear.

"Give me a status."

There was a short silence.

"Good. You can land on the junction. That's our only option. But it will have to happen fast. I am willing to give up one truck at the most; everything else will have to be out of here before the army arrives... I don't care! We probably have three to four hours, just get it started."

It was decided that all trucks be on their way and take the left turnoff at the junction. At least that way no time was being lost. It would take them longer to get to the border, and there would be other problems to face, but they'd deal with that later.

Meanwhile Auguste Fitzgeraldo and some of his men would wait at the junction for the arrival of a couple of helicopters. They would fly the contents of the two stranded trucks out of here, or as much as they could. The rest could be hidden in the thick foliage of the forest.

"Isn't this everything you've always dreamed of, señor Pappas?" said Fitzgeraldo. "A chase. An army in pursuit. A bank heist. And a last-minute escape through the air? You will find your next business talk on the radio quite boring, I expect."

"I was born to do that kind of work, it will never be boring. You're the one who's bored here. When will enough be enough for people like you?"

"Never, I suppose. Because as soon as that happens, I'll start to be bored. So I guess it all makes sense."

"I still don't see why you want me to go along," sighed Carl. "Do you really believe the army of Corazón will hold their fire just because you are standing behind me? They're a junta! They care as little about hostages as you do."

"On the contrary! And you yourself have proven that. Haven't you befriended one of the junta leaders within a few hours after your arrival in Corazón? I am very confident your newfound *amigo* will do his utmost to protect such a famous friend. The government of Corazón will be delighted to have such a powerful ally as the Bizz Jockey from now on. They protect you, they rescue you and you will speak favorably of them forevermore."

"You are a cunning man, Fitzgeraldo. You'd make a fine guest on my show," said Carl. "I need people who can make strong arguments, it's good for the ratings."

Fitzgeraldo laughed. "You see? You should be grateful. When this is all over, your ratings will skyrocket."

"Unless... I have an accident in this jungle."

"That, I agree, is always a danger. But I think that as long as I am safe, you will be safe with me, Mr. Pappas." He coughed and coughed, and his head turned all red.

"It looks to me that greed is not the only virus you are taking across the border," said Carl. "Don't you think you should surrender to the army and get treatment before this fever kills you like it killed your driver? Look at yourself!"

"You'd like that, wouldn't you," moaned Fitzgerald, who had a sudden attack from whatever ailment was tormenting him. "And then tell the world that I got killed by my own greed. Come on, say it, you think greed is a virus that needs to be exterminated!"

"Oh, get a life," said Carl. "Just because I am arguing against paying zero taxes doesn't mean I have a problem with greed. Go ahead and be as greedy as you want, I don't care. You can have it!"

"Good," said Fitzgerald, who seemed to be regaining control over his fever. "I'm glad we got that out of the way. Now if you will excuse me, I have to oversee the operations. In a few moments the helicopters will start their work. You and I will be on the last flight."

Auguste walked to the door, and turned back one more time. "Or you and I will be dead in the mud."

Fifteen

As soon as Auguste Fitzgeraldo had left the small building on the Plato Grosso junction, all hell broke loose. Carl was still seated on the chair in the room that was now completely empty, but for himself and the dead driver, and completely dark. He heard the sound of approaching helicopters. They were appearing out of nowhere, right above the junction.

Carl jumped up. He felt he had to do something.

Then shooting was added to the tumult. There was the rattling of machine guns and there were explosions.

Carl turned away from the door and ran to the back of the small building, stumbling among chairs and crates. Touching the wall he found a window. He jerked it open and felt a wooden shutter blocking his way out from the outside. He started pounding the wood.

"I'm gettin' out of here nów," he yelled in an attempt to boost his spirits, to crank up his adrenalin level. He turned his head in the direction where he suspected the corpse lay on one of the bunks: "You can take that chopper!"

The small building shuddered from the impact of an explosion nearby and Carl was not making any progress.

Behind him the door was kicked open and someone yelled: "Carl Evangelos Pappas! You in here?"

He recognized Hitomi's voice. As he turned around, a flashlight blinded him.

"I'm here!"

"Carl Evangelos Pappas, you... You..." yelled Hitomi.

Then she had her arms around the bizz jockey and hugged him. She flashed a light and checked him out. "Are you hurt?"

"I can function," said Carl. "Got a couple of bruises and a dead man."

Hitomi flashed the light around. "I see what you mean."

They walked to the door and watched the junction, which had turned into a war zone.

A helicopter had been hit and had crashed into one of the two remaining trucks. A fire was consuming whatever was inside the truck and there was no longer any rain to stop it. While a jet fighter roared across the junction, there was a whole circus of shooting going on. From under and behind the second gold truck, Fitzgeraldo's men were firing at several army vehicles that stood in the road leading from Caribal. From behind these vehicles the fire was returned vehemently.

"The man responsible for all this, is right over there," said Carl in the blazing noise. He pointed at a shady figure that was moving in the light of the flames, about to disappear into the jungle.

Carl started running, keeping his head low, in pursuit of Auguste Fitzgeraldo.

"Pappas, what are you..." yelled Hitomi.

And then she murmured: "I can't believe this."

She started running after him, shouting: "This has no editorial value whatsoever, Carl! Let that man go!"

But of course her boss paid no attention. He ran straight across the junction, away from all the military action, to the place where one of the paths led into the jungle, vaguely lit by the light emanating from the burning truck. Hitomi ran as fast as she could and caught up with him, pointing her flashlight ahead of them on the path.

"Are you insane? These people have guns, Carl," she panted.

"He's alone, Hitomi. I saw it. That's Auguste Fitzgeraldo and he's unarmed. He leaves the dirty work to his thugs and now he's running. We can catch up with him, he has no more of a stomach for survival in the jungle than I have."

"Who cares? We need to get out of here."

"He is the only man who knows where all that money will end up. If we keep him from running away, we have a huge news story for The Boardroom. It will be a major case in the fight against tax evasion... errr... pfff." Carl's condition was not up to all this.

They both ran for a while. They could both feel the small path was leading them down to somewhere lower in the jungle, possibly the river Coramazon.

"Let's at least go back and get some help, Carl."

"Forget it. It's now or never. If we go back, he'll disappear in a forest bigger than Japan."

"Leave Japan out of this, Carl Evangelos Pappas," said Hitomi.

===

Colonel Rhodes puffed his cigar. He banged shoulders with his comrades from the army. Then he rounded up a few soldiers. The shooting had stopped.

"Search the entire junction," he barked, "and that includes the surrounding area and that building. I came here with Miss Hitomi Sakamoto and somehow I can't find her now. I have reason to believe she is missing along with Auguste Fitzgeraldo and Carl Pappas. On the double! And someone get me a flashlight before that fire goes out and we are in the dark again! I want to be able to smell fear!"

Sixteen

It was only a matter of time before Carl Pappas started to have second thoughts about their pursuit of Auguste Fitzgeraldo. Hitomi had been right: it was a dangerous endeavor, and they were up against a cunning man with a knack for survival. Suddenly he remembered that it had been Auguste Fitzgeraldo who had tossed Mach One's middle man from the cliffs to his death in the bay, and no one else. Even if he had ordered one of his bodyguards to perform the task, Fitzgeraldo was still a ruthless adversary. There was no turning back now, but they would have to be extremely careful.

They slowed down.

"I'm out of breath," said Carl. "So he'll be out of breath too."

"You assume too much," whispered Hitomi.

"I'm not giving up on that man." Carl started to whisper now too, but he also started to sound less secure.

"The only reason I allow you to continue this pursuit," whispered Hitomi, "is that Colonel Rhodes will send his men in all directions, including the path we're on. There's only two paths to check anyway since the other paths lead in the wrong direction. They'll catch up with us very soon. If we proceed cautiously, they will be here before we run into that Fitzgeraldo."

Carl wanted to respond, but he didn't have the breath for it. They walked for a while, Hitomi pointing the flashlight towards the ground. The jungle had closed above them and surrounded them like a tunnel. A black tunnel.

After three quarters of an hour — Carl felt like two hours had passed — they arrived at a clearing in the forest. The last half hour the path had become steep, leading them straight down to this open place by a river. He and Hitomi had started running again the last couple of hundred meters in an attempt to gain some terrain on their prey. They were more successful than they had bargained for.

Because all of a sudden they stood on this open spot by the river, and while they made a quick assessment of the area — an open circle by the water about fifty meters in diameter, a small river with a powerful stream of water, and a path that ran alongside it — they heard a sarcastic laugh emerging behind them.

They turned and looked right into the beam of a powerful flashlight. Their sight was entirely blinded.

"Don't raise your flashlight, please," said the voice of Auguste Fitzgerald. "I have a gun."

They heard a clicking noise that might or might not have come from a gun. They simply couldn't tell, but the point was made.

"So here we are," said Auguste, "for the final confrontation.

Do you have anything to say to make me feel better, Pappas? And who is she?"

"None of your business," hissed Hitomi.

"I made you an offer, Fitzgeraldo," said Carl. "There is still time for you to take it. You arrange that your clients make a better deal with their own countries, and I skip the whole item on my radio show."

"But you have absolutely NOTHING to substantiate that!" shouted Fitzgerald. "I had all that business running smoothly. Nobody cared. Not the government of Corazón. Not the governments of the USA, Russia, China, Japan or any European government for that matter. They all left us alone. All these big shots parked their money here through the channels I alone created. Until you arrived. Until your man started hacking the bank and downloaded all these names and account numbers and information about assets."

Carl looked around him. The light was too blinding. He saw nothing. Not a sound was coming from the jungle. There was only the powerful rushing of the small river. "You did a nice job disposing yourself of that man and that information."

"I did, didn't I? But by that time it was too late. Too many people were becoming suspicious. How do I know he didn't leak some of that stuff to some governments? Anyway, things were stirred that should have been left alone. I did the only thing that I could do: ship the money out of Corazón before it was too late. Everything for my clients."

"Good for you, Fitzgeraldo. There's still time to make it right."

"Screw you, Pappas. There's no way back now. But I owe it to my clients to get rid of the world's greatest enemy of any tax paradise."

There was that clicking sound again.

"Now wait," Hitomi began.

There was a rushing sound, then a roaring sound, then a large thud and finally high-pitch screaming. At the same time the beam of the flashlight started to move around wildly.

It was instantly clear that Auguste Fitzgeraldo had engaged in a life and death struggle with a large inhabitant of the tropical rainforest. From all this wild movement in the jumping beam of the flashlight they could make out the spotted skin of some large cat moving. They could also hear some of the animal's grumbling. But they couldn't make anything out of Fitzgerald's high pitch screamed words. It was gibberish.

"It's a tiger!" hollered Carl.

Then a shot rang out. A bullet found it's way into the foliage surrounding the open spot.

"Dive!" shouted Hitomi, "He's firing the gun! And there are no tigers here. It must be a jaguar."

Carl and Hitomi threw themselves to the ground to be out of the way.

"A jaguar, that's a relief! We have to help him, Sakamoto!"

"I know that!"

He heard her get up on her feet, but before Carl could act, another shot rang, Hitomi screamed, there was a lot of rushing and clattering of leaves. Then it was silent. Only the rushing of the river and the panting of Hitomi remained. But there was no more gunfire. Nor could the jaguar be heard.

Hitomi shone her flashlight.

A motionless body lay in the mud close to the bushes and the trees. There was no sight of the jaguar.

Then she pointed the flashlight at her arm. "Carl Evangelos Pappas!"

"Now what?"

"I've been shot."

Seventeen

The tropical sun courted the little forest village for a few minutes.

Then it attacked full force.

All but one, they were sitting by the river, a few miles from where Auguste Fitzgeraldo had died at the claws of the jaguar. Behind them the small river gave way to a larger reservoir, that stretched a couple of hundred meters in diameter, and allowed the sun to shine on the modest assembly of huts so early in the day. A helicopter stood in the center of the village. The local people, a friendly, indigenous tribe, walked around barefoot. They wore jeans and sunglasses, and a ghetto blaster performed its torturous task from the riverside. None of them was even remotely interested in the small invasion that had temporarily taken place. Nor were they listening to the ranting of Phil Solo, who stood towering over Carl Pappas. During the time Phil spoke, the words seem to come out of his mouth in a pace that resembled that of the river. Thanks to the heavy rainfall of the previous night the small stream had turned into a powerful current.

Even in the middle of this tropical rainforest, with

mosquitos flying around in abundance, mud splattering up with every step, leaves of grass and bushes and trees reaching out from all around you to touch and stain you, Phil Solo maintained the kind of corporate coolness that made him the envy of many people — though certainly not of Carl Pappas and Don Wozniak — and the target of many women. His dark suit was spotless and, even after a helicopter flight, without wrinkles. His hair was waxed backwards like a younger version of John Travolta, a light moving and energetic man, sure of himself but in a perpetual fight with colleagues who he perceived to be subversive. He was suspected of arguing even in his sleep. There was probably not a single member of the editorial team of The Boardroom who could cherish a single moment of friendliness from their uberboss, Phil Solo. True, the Bizz Jockey could be grumpy, but at least he was also a man of jokes and banter.

"I give up," said Solo finally, after he had exhausted himself and had started to detect a certain repetitive pattern in his speech. "Right now I feel like firing everybody. Which of course I'll regret within minutes, but nevertheless. Capiche? Well, at least I'll feel good for an instant!"

"Thank you for your speech, Phil," said Carl. "I really appreciate that. But there is no need for it. Why don't you just say that you were going through hell, worrying about our safety? That's nothing to be ashamed of."

"I am not," said Phil, "I repeat I am nót going to repeat how running after a dangerous lunatic in the jungle, with armed soldiers running after you, who could mistake you for someone they'd love to shoot, is extremely irresponsible. Why you, Sakamoto, have gone along with this nonsense is beyond me. Under normal circumstances you are the only reasonable person on the entire Boardroom staff!" He threw his hands in the air and sat down. "There! I get carried away again. Like I said: I give up."

Carl Pappas threw a dead branch into the river. Then he got up to find another branch and threw a couple more. "I am not going to argue with you, Phil. Of course it is all insane. We've had a rough twenty-four hours, one thing led to another. Who can think straight when you fall over dead bodies while waterskiing? Who can focus in the midst of exploding buildings, helicopters crashing into trucks full of money, tsunamis of rain beating down on you and tigers emerging from the jungle hungry for human flesh!"

"Jaguars," said Hitomi. Her left arm was wrapped in a bandage.

"Everybody, there is no need to be upset!" yelled Colonel Rhodes. He was approaching them from the center of the village. "You are all safe now. Why quarrel? I propose we all sail back to Caribal in the boat that will be here in half an hour."

"Can't we just fly back?" said Hitomi. "You have helicopters. We need to get back fast, we have a live radio show to prepare and we have lost a lot of time."

"Oh take it easy, Hitomi," said Carl. "Maybe we should just cancel it. You know, the data I was going to come up with, there's none of that anymore. It's all gone. Besides, you're injured. You are going to hospital. You don't want to catch some tropical disease here, with that wound."

"No way, Pappas," said Hitomi while she rushed to her feet. "The show must go on. We have plenty of other stuff. We also have live guests. We can't quit! I won't have it."

Colonel Rhodes put an arm around Hitomi's shoulder. He was a much bigger man than the small Japanese radio producer. Even Phil Solo had to smile at the sight of Hitomi trying to get away from underneath the Colonel's arm.

"This woman has impressed me for life," barked Colonel Rhodes. "She is an example for any revolutionary. Steady as a rock, energetic like a hurricane, and fearless in the face of the enemy. Look, she even got shot. That's more than I can say. We can use someone like you, Miss Sakamoto. You'd be a fine icon for the position of women in our society. How about I offer you a job as Secretary of the Interior of Corazón?"

Finally Hitomi got loose. "You are most gracious, Colonel. But I have a job to do. The helicopter, please?"

The Colonel made a gesture towards one of the military standing around. "Go with that man, please, Miss Sakamoto. Your wish is my command."

He winked at Carl and Phil.

"I'll join her," said Solo as he got up. "I do not wish to be here another minute. I'm leaving some WCBN security personnel behind with Mr. Pappas, if that's all right, Colonel."

He got his acknowledgement through a wave of Rhodes' hand. A gracious gesture that could not be misunderstood: request granted.

As Phil Solo marched off after Hitomi Sakamoto, Colonel Rhodes sat down with Carl. "You are a fortunate man, *amigo*. You have friends to watch over you. Everybody here is your friend. And the one who is not, is dead. You lucky man."

"I hope I have not upset your government too much," said Carl. "It seems that our presence here has stirred things up way beyond expectation."

And yes, the cigars came out again.

After he had lit one, puffing away, the Colonel replied: "It was only a matter of time before the diverting and hiding of money through our banking system was going to become an international problem, *amigo*. You have speeded things up a little. So what? Like I told you before, the Republic of Corazón is very, very anxious to take a more prominent position on the world stage. A man of your stature, being in Caribal, broadcasting about our financial position, can only help! I've explained that to my fellow statesmen. We are all aware that it may be a little rough for a while, but in the long run it will be for the better."

Carl looked across the water.

"Your boat will take you and me to Caribal in a couple of hours. We will have plenty of time to discuss the matter and I will tell you all you need to know for your program."

"There's one other thing," said Carl. "That guy, that Fitzgeraldo, he picked up a fever from his driver. I think you should look into it. What if it's a highly contagious thing? Some of his other men have driven on and will cross the border. You don't want an epidemic on your hands."

"The military doctor has checked them out and it was just a jungle fever. A coincidence, nothing more."

Carl felt he was now being scrutinized to the max. The Colonel looked at him with piercing eyes.

"You are not going to... mention this on the radio?"

It's a military junta after all, he thought. Keep that in mind.

"If you say so, *amigo*," he said.

The Colonel hit him on the shoulder so hard that, for a

moment, Carl worried about a possible bone fracture.

"Finally you acknowledge that you also have friends in this country," said Rhodes. "You are a stubborn man, Mr. Pappas. But not that stubborn, eh?"

Eighteen

The unfamiliar environment of the Caribal Radio studio had been efficiently changed for the better. Don Wozniak had filled the space with his usual music, remarks and clutter, as well as he could, with his right hand all wrapped up in Band-Aid. As soon as Hitomi walked in, the sound of the Rod Steward song "Passion" filled the room. Even the sturdy little Japanese producer laughed this time.

Don started a message, one he had recorded before hand and downloaded for the occasion.

It was the anonymous WCBN Radio voice, announcing: "It's eleven o'clock. Outside's it's beginning to cool down after a tropical day in the Republic of Corazón, but here in the studio of Corazón Radio the temperatures are about to rise again. Because in the midst of delusion and truth your prophet, the buddy and bodyguard of ever man and woman in business, will fill another episode of The Boardroom. Not everybody is going to be amused. Still, what's not to like about the man, the world's one and only bizz jockey. Here he is, your BJ: Carl Pappas!"

"That's all very well, people," Carl kicked off, "but the heat was becoming unbearable here. So I for one am glad that the night is falling and we can all sit down in one of the last studios in the world where a man can smoke a proper cigar without someone suing him. So that couldn't be better, because with me is a cigar connoisseur and enlightened statesman, he is our special guest tonight. May I introduce to you: Colonel Rhodes of the Corazón administration! Welcome to The Boardroom, Colonel, where just like any other day we ask ourselves: where do we stand? If you know the answer, you may call now. But don't take this lightly; many went before you. Many were mistaken. And are grounded now, in court, in jail or in hell. A few moments from now I will slap Colonel Rhodes on the shoulder and get him to talk about some pretty innarestin' stuff. But first... And yes, we have our first caller. This is Carl Pappas in The Boardroom, can I help you?"

"Well hello Mr. Pappas, it's Secretary Hector Kopenhagen for you," a familiar voice sounded.

"Mr. Secretary, what a pleasant surprise. I have a feeling I know why you're calling!"

"You've won by a landslide, Carl," said the Secretary. "You have just done something that would otherwise have taken many years to accomplish. You have singlehandedly terminated the largest money pit in the civilized world. In the very near future a lot of taxes will be coming our way. You're a man of miraculous talents."

Meanwhile, Hitomi Sakamoto stood quietly, watching, reminiscing the dangers her boss had been through, and the comradery it had created. Hell, she had even smiled at the sound engineer. She had to work on getting a stronger grip on her emotions, she decided. This was work, not some gathering of friends.

Look at me, she thought. My thoughts are rambling during the show. I'm not hearing a thing. I'm pathetic. It must be the tropics.

===

Finally the bizz jockey lowered his voice a bit, while Don Wozniak arranged for a moody, jazzy piano sound in the background. "Bad manners can be like a virus, they spread," said Carl into the microphone that carried his voice away from here, across the globe. "I've seen viruses like that at work and I can assure you: they can kill you."

Colonel Rhodes, leaning backwards comfortably in his chair, frowned at these words.

The Bizz Jockey continued: "Hiding your money from taxes is considered bad manners by your fellow citizens. I am not the man to address any of you people about this topic. It is your personal responsibility. It is not the duty of governments to berate you for it. Listen, making things right is a small step for you, but it's a major boost for your country's economy. I hope tonight's show has given you a new perspective on this issue, and more understanding of other people's position on this. Regardless of how yóu act from now on."

It was a small space, nothing like the large WCBN Radio studio, and Hitomi stood so close to the Bizz Jockey, he could actually reach out and touch her hand.

And that's precisely what he did, much to the embarrassment of Hitomi.

"We've talked about Corazón and how it's rising to the challenge of a new world, a new type of economic future. I can tell you: it is also a mysterious country, and there are forces at work here that are life saving. I am a personal witness to that. It may look to you like we're just doing our jobs here, and earning our money, but sometimes it's just not about money. And you can quote me on that!"

***

Request from the author

Thank you for reading this Radio Detective adventure. I hope you enjoyed it and will be willing to write a review on the online platform of your choice. Making that extra effort is greatly appreciated by other readers... and of course by me. Thank you.

I hope you and I stay connected through Twitter, Facebook, Google+, Pinterest or my free email newsletter. I'll make sure you'll stay tuned.

Have a good evening/night/day!

M.H. Vesseur

Twitter @MHVesseur

Facebook www.facebook.com/MHVesseur

Subscribe to M.H. Vesseur's mailing list on www.mhvesseur.com

About the author

M.H. Vesseur has written many short stories for literary magazines in The Netherlands, Belgium, Canada and the U.S.A. He was awarded for the best debut with his first story. In his radio detective series about Carl Pappas he has now written and published the seven short crime novels *CEO Groupie*, *Die Rich*, *Tax Me If You Can*, *Acid Asset*, *Nosedive*, *Power Play* and *Blood Border*. The radio detective's producer Hitomi Sakamoto now stars in her own series, which begins with *North*. M.H. Vesseur also published the novel *Lemniscate*, a collection of literary short stories called *Allusions* and his outlook on the super economy *Burning Neil Armstrong*. M.H. Vesseur is an awarded advertising copywriter. He lives in the forests of The Netherlands.

www.mhvesseur.com

Novels and ebooks by M.H. Vesseur
More information on:
www.mhvesseur.com/publications

Allusions (short story collection)
North (The Hitomi Files: 1)
Blood Border (a Radio Detective novel)
Power Play (a Radio Detective novel)
Nosedive (a Radio Detective novel)
Acid Asset (a Radio Detective novel)
Tax Me If You Can (a Radio Detective novel)
Die Rich (a Radio Detective novel)
CEO Groupie (a Radio Detective novel)
Beloved Stalker
Babyface Junkie
In Snuff Park
Sketches Of A Worldwide Christo And Jeanne-Claude
Narcissist Guru
Territory Game

Short stories by M.H. Vesseur

ALLUSIONS

Glimpses of tomorrow await you in this collection. The ultimate amusement park will offer you death. Everlasting youth will take you to the point of no return. The artificial landscape will fill you with joy if it doesn't scare the living daylights out of you. The Narcissist Guru will show you your many selves. There is the ultimate work of art that will change the planet and the old vaudeville star who is still being stalked. And finally, the coming of the super economy will haunt your dreams. This collection contains the short stories • In Snuff Park • Babyface Junkie • Narcissist Guru • Sketches of a Worldwide Christo and Jeanne-Claude • Territory Game • Beloved Stalker • Burning Neil Armstrong.

Available in The Hitomi Files by M.H. Vesseur

NORTH

Man should fear only one enemy

The only enemy who has the capacity to remove all of mankind from the earth, is the virus. Imagine the worst of them all, a true 21st century killer. It lies dormant in the remote laboratory of a pharmaceutical giant whose hopes of making billions off a vaccine somewhere in the future throw a dark shadow ahead. Then Hitomi Sakamoto, the hard boiled radio producer who's on a rough vacation in the wild nature of the north, stumbles upon this dark secret. She is drawn into a final battle between ruthless scientists, a greedy corporation, desperate but dangerous environmental activists, a cold-hearted assassin and... a manmade virus that longs to escape.

Hitomi Sakamoto first appeared in the Radio Detective novels by

M.H. Vesseur. Immediately popular for her iron work ethics and razorsharp tongue, Hitomi outgrew her boss (radio detective Carl Pappas) and now steps out of his shadow, into her very own adventure.

Available in the radio detective series by M.H. Vesseur

CEO GROUPIE - A radio detective novel

One night three live guests join Carl Pappas on his radio show The Boardroom: two CEOs and a woman who calls herself: "the CEO Groupie". When the mysterious woman reveals the existence of a secret call girl organization for CEOs and subsequently disappears a couple of days later, the bizz jockey engages on a search. What happened to the CEO Groupie and what are the other two guests up to? Together with his radio team — his producer Hitomi Sakamoto and his sound engineer Don Wozniak — Carl Pappas sets out to deal with this.

Available in the radio detective series by M.H. Vesseur

DIE RICH - A radio detective novel

Carl Pappas, the bizz jockey, goes on the air again. His radio show "The Boardroom" is both loved and feared by the global business community. He has a sharp eye for business news and the big mouth of a talk radio host. This time around he has some very wealthy guests joining him on his show: two billionaire entrepeneurs and their future successors, who also happen to be their sons. Of course it doesn't take the bizz jockey a very long time to upset some of his guests and his audience — and that same night the bizz jockey finds himself heading into dangerous waters, in the hands of some very angry rich people. His team — producer Hitomi Sakamoto and sound engineer Don Wozniak — is forced to go out and rescue their reckless boss. And then there are the rich kids they have to deal with...

Available in the radio detective series by M.H. Vesseur

ACID ASSET - A radio detective novel

Carl Pappas, the bizz jockey, is feeling good about the prospects of environment-friendly plastics he's discussing on his radio show "The Boardroom". But as he soon finds out there's something not right with the company behind it. Can the bizz jockey protect a lonely scientist against the schemes of a large corporation that smells money? Or will he be unable to stop a revolutionary asset from becoming really acidic? Buckle up for a race against arsonists, corporate crime, dogs, bullets and a dangerous industrial zone in the middle of a blizzard, softened only by some real team spirit.

Also available in the radio detective series

NOSEDIVE - A radio detective novel

When a large corporation is struck by a cripling strike among its workers and an apparent terrorist attack on its factory, bizz jockey Carl Pappas steps forward to offer his public support. But as he soon finds out, there's more to the picture than meets the eye. Why is the owner hiding in her large mansion? What happened in her youth that is threatening her after all these years? It's a job for the radio detective — and this time around his boss gives an unexpected hand.

Available in the radio detective series by M.H. Vesseur

POWER PLAY - A radio detective novel

The death of an environmental activist brings bizz jockey and unofficial "radio detective" Carl Pappas to the quiet island of Islasol. Everything seems to be OK with the local National Park and the wind turbine park in the heart of it.

But Carl and his team soon find out you can't take anything on face value. Below the surface of an environment friendly enterprise lies a darker secret. It's time for the radio detective to unravel the local secrets of wind energy, assisted by his producer Hitomi and a new, unlikely ally.

Available in the radio detective series by M.H. Vesseur

BLOOD BORDER - A radio detective novel

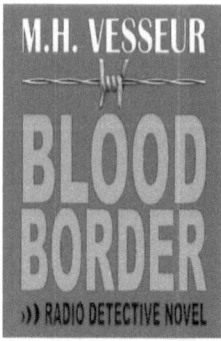

The inhumanity of human trafficking is forcing the radio detective to make a stand. So in the midst of politics and public outrage, Carl Pappas and his team infiltrate the trafficking cartel of a man known as The Clown. But there is nothing funny about it, for the radio detective soon finds himself in the lion's den, a place crowded with former narcotics traffickers and their violent ways. Will they be able to do something about the screaming injustice of immigration or will they become prey themselves?

<<<<>>>>